ELLA AND THE MULTIVERSE

ANDREW S. FRENCH

NEONOIR BOOKS

Book one: Don't Fear the Reaper

Book two: The Killing Moon

Book three: Lost in America

Book four: Gone to Texas

The Detective Jen Flowers series

Book one: The Hashtag Killer

Book two: Serial Killer

Book three: Night Killer

Book four: The Killer Inside Them

Northern Crime Fiction

Where The Bodies Are Buried

Crime Short Stories

Call Me: An Astrid Snow Short Story

Dark Snow: An Astrid Snow Short Story

Go to www.andrewsfrench.com for more information.

1 WHITE RABBIT

It was the end of the beginning when Ella peered at the towering grass in front of her. It shimmered and swayed from side to side, covered in purple flowers that smelt of lavender. When she'd stepped through the door which separated her world from this one, she'd wondered how she'd know it was another dimension, but it didn't take that long. The six-foot-tall rabbit striding towards her might have given it away, and she was impressed with the bright red suit he wore, but the giant pair of human eyes staring at her from the sky clinched it.

'Don't worry about that. It's only your future self checking to see if you're okay.' The rabbit held out one paw to her while the other gripped a mobile phone. 'My name is Jack.'

Ella moved back an inch. 'You're Jack, the rabbit?'

He withdrew his paw and pulled a carrot from his jacket pocket. He nibbled on it as he spoke.

'What's a rabbit?'

She glanced around her, seeing the sea and a beach to

the right of the grass. It reminded Ella of home and what she'd left behind.

'Where am I?'

The giant rabbit finished his meal. 'Here? This is Everywhere.'

The eyes in the sky continued to peer at her, so she peered back. There was something in them which made her think the rabbit's claim might be true. Could that be a version of her in the clouds? A week ago, she'd have thought such a thing ridiculous, but after discovering the Book of All Life and that Elementals existed, she doubted nothing anymore.

Ella offered her hand. 'I'm pleased to meet you, Jack.'

The rabbit grinned and took her hand. His fur was warm against her skin.

'The feeling is mutual, Ella.'

She let go of him. 'How do you know who I am?'

He swivelled on his feet, pointed the phone into the air, and snapped a photo of the giant eyes.

'Your future self told me you'd be here. I'm to be your guide in Everywhere.'

Butterflies fluttered in Ella's heart. 'That's me up there?'

He sneaked another carrot into his mouth. 'It's one version of you.' As he said that, the eyes disappeared. 'It will all become clear as we go.'

'Will it?'

He bellowed out a hearty human laugh. 'Probably not, no. But we won't know unless we try, will we?'

Ella remembered why she was there, wherever this Everywhere was.

'I'm searching for Pandora. Do you know her?'

Jack scratched at his chin. 'I don't speak to strangers.

But I took some photos of recent visitors who travelled through the same gateway you did.'

He handed her the phone and she was surprised to see it was the same make and model as hers.

Ella found the images straight away, flicking through half a dozen creatures she'd never seen before, even in books or films. A horse with six legs, a woman with fire for hair, a man made of stone, a floating ball of ice with the face of a cat, and a fierce beast with teeth bigger than its head. Then she saw the photos of Pandora, three of them of the person who used to be her friend Dora, looking old and scared as she headed towards the sea.

Ella returned the phone to the rabbit.

'I need to find her. Can you show me where she went?'

'Following her is easy. Finding where she went is something else.'

She glanced around her as the dirt grumbled beneath her feet.

'What do you mean?'

'As I told you before, this is Everywhere. Which means it leads to every dimension in existence. Be careful where you walk, as anything can be a doorway to another realm.' He pointed to the spot where Ella had entered. 'You and this Pandora came through the same door, but after that, she could have exited through any gateway.'

Ella thought about what he'd said. She'd watched a movie once about something called the multiverse. That must be what the rabbit meant.

'Couldn't Pandora still be here?'

He furrowed his brow. 'She might, but this is just one, never-ending corridor. The only things that hang around here are the bad ones waiting to pounce on the unsuspecting.'

The ground moved beneath them again.

'Pandora is bad.'

Jack dropped bits of carrot at his feet. 'Tell me more about this person.'

Before she could reply, something moved underneath the dirt, and then disappeared. Ella tried to cram all she knew into a few sentences, concerned about what was moving beneath her feet.

'Pandora claims to have created every living thing on my planet, Earth. This includes humans like me and Elementals, which we thought were mythological creatures like unicorns, witches and dragons. She said the humans feared her, so thousands of years ago in our time, they tricked her, so she banished all the Elementals, and herself, into a realm they couldn't escape from. Yet, over the centuries, gaps have appeared between the realms, and a few slipped through. Humanity's meddling with the climate has weakened the barrier to the point of collapse. Pandora found a way back to Earth, intending to enslave all humans. Until I stopped her.'

Jack looked at Ella with admiration covering his hairy face.

'How did you do that?'

She told him about the Book of All Life and how she used it to bring Elementals to help her on Earth. And she told him about Light.

Jack nodded. 'I know what that is.' He placed one hand over his heart. 'We call it the Glow. It's the essence which leaves our bodies when we die, and then travels to the next realm.'

She wanted to ask him so many questions, but the mud thrust against her shoes like a giant burp and she nearly fell over.

'What's happening?'

He grabbed her hand and pulled her towards the sea.

'The snarks are getting restless and my bits of carrot aren't enough to keep them happy. We have to leave now.'

She ran with him as the ground growled around them like an upset stomach. The wind bit at her ears as the smell of salt water rushed towards her. Ella gripped Jack's paw.

'What's a snark?'

He stopped when they reached the sand. 'We should be safe here. Snarks don't like the water.' He let go of her. 'Snarks feed on other living creatures, but they have to upset you first.'

A wave ran over her shoes and dripped into her socks.

'That doesn't sound very terrible, having to upset you.'

Jack lowered his head to her and she noticed he had different coloured eyes. One was deep blue, while the other was a mix of red and yellow.

'Are you a tough girl, Ella? Do you weep when people call you names?'

She stuck out her chest. 'My parents disappeared and I didn't cry.' But she'd wanted to. 'Then I had to live with my aunt and uncle, who were terrible to me and made me live in a barn with the animals. Their three daughters, my cousins, picked on me every day. None of that made me cry. And I had to watch as my friend Dora turned into Pandora and told me I was her relative and what horrible things she was going to do to the world. After all that, I never cried once.'

Jack nodded. 'Good, Ella. You'll need all of that strength with what's ahead of you.'

Before she could ask what he meant, the dirt burst from the ground like an exploding volcano. Mud and grass went everywhere and she saw worms thrown into the air. Before they could fall, a large head like a snake's thrust up and gobbled dirt and worms alike. As it ate them up, it howled like a wolf.

Ella's feet were frozen into the sand as the creature turned to her.

'The furball lies to you, child. It's only here to lure you to its lair where it will boil you alive before feeding you to its family.'

The creature's breath stank of mould and damp, while its yellowed teeth gnashed at her.

'Why should I believe you?'

The snark spat bits of worm at her feet.

'You're a stupid little girl far from home. You lost your parents, and then you abandoned them to run away when you found them again. You're small, and you smell, and something will eat you soon.'

'How do you know about my parents?'

It lowered its head, with slimy scales close to her face and the stink of death escaping from its mouth.

'I know everything about you, Ella Finn. You can't hide anything from me, child. All your friends leave you and your parents don't love you. Pandora didn't kidnap them. They went with her willingly to get away from you. You're alone because everyone hates you.'

She pushed her face close to the snark, feeling its sweat dripping on to her cheeks.

'That's a lie. I've got a friend called Billy.'

'Yes, poor old Billy Pudding. You left him behind as well, just like you did with your mum and dad.' Its tongue slithered out of its mouth and over its lips. 'And now there's no one to protect them.'

Heat exploded through Ella's veins. 'Protect them from what?'

'Pandora double-crossed you, child. She's returned to your home with her Elementals, and all is lost for you there.' Its face touched hers, the slime of its flesh seeping into her skin. 'There's only one thing which can save them now.'

She pulled back from it as a wave washed over her feet. That's when she saw Jack lying in the water. She dropped to her knees, hitting wet sand as she dragged him up. His curious eyes were glazed over as he choked. She'd seen a video once of someone saving a drowning man, so she knew what to do.

Ella put her lips over his and sucked liquid from Jack's lungs. She gave it one huge gulp before letting go and spitting the water back into the sea. Jack didn't move, so she did it again. After the third try, he gasped and water splashed out of his mouth. His eyes were fuzzy, but he was breathing normally. She held on to him as she turned to the snark.

'What have you done to him?'

The snake-like creature laughed at her, a terrible sound that sent a shiver down Ella's spine.

'Why, child, only what I've done to you.' Its slimy neck pushed further out of the ground and it slithered towards her. 'I'm in his head like I'm in yours. If you give in to me, everything will be fine, and your parents and your friend and your world will survive.'

She glanced at Jack in the sand, feeling the water covering her shoes and trickling between her toes.

'None of this is real.'

The snark twisted towards her. 'It is to you and him, child.'

'Is that so?' She stared at her palm and imagined a knife in her hand. It appeared in an instant. Then she took it and jabbed it into the snark's slimy neck.

The creature howled and reeled from her, its head

shaking as if it was in a microwave. Green blood sputtered from the wound and into the sea, turning the orange sand into a dirty black.

Then Ella blinked and it all disappeared, replaced with what was real. The snark lay dead, with no sign of a wound or any blood. She no longer had the knife, and Jack stood next to her.

'We have to go, Ella. The others will be angry now and out for revenge.'

She stared at the thing she'd killed with her mind.

'The others?'

He grabbed her hand. 'The rest of the snarks. They always travel in packs. If more than one comes, they'll over-whelm us.' He looked at the dead snark. 'Even though you're stronger than you look.'

As he said that, the earth behind them shook like an earthquake. Jack pulled her towards the water as a thousand wild howls shattered the quiet.

'You're dragging us into the sea,' Ella shouted.

He glanced at her as they ran through the waves.

'No, that's where we're going.'

They stopped and he let go of her to point at the gap between the sand and the sea. If they'd been standing on a cliff, it would have been the edge. As the noise increased behind them, she inched towards the gap, bending her head to peer into an abyss.

'How is this possible?'

Jack shrugged. 'Everything is possible in Everywhere, Ella.'

His eyes sparkled as she turned towards the howling. A dozen giant snakeheads slithered towards them, their yellowed teeth snapping away. She had about twenty seconds to decide: the marauding snarks' teeth or the impossible gap between the sand and the sea.

It was no choice at all.

2 LET'S DANCE

Ella didn't know how long she fell for, but it seemed to go on forever. It was pitch black at first, so dark she could hardly tell if she was falling at all. There was no sensation of movement, no draughts or wind against her skin, and no feeling gravity had abandoned her. There were no sounds or smells, either; no touch of Jack, even though she'd held on to the tall rabbit as they'd jumped into the abyss together.

She remembered once, a long time ago, when she was playing a game with her parents and hid from them in the cupboard under the stairs. It had been dark there, but not like this. Then there had been glints of light through the door, and she'd touched the things in there with her: coats and jackets, slippers and shoes, and the few toys she'd given up as she got older, such as the fluffy dog and the squeaky mouse.

Now there was no sensation but the darkness. She tried to move her legs and arms, but couldn't.

It stinks of burning rubber.

She went to touch her nose, but nothing moved. Or perhaps it did and she couldn't feel it.

Ella was ready to think she was dead when someone switched the sun on. The light was so brilliant, it hurt her eyes. Now she was falling, but only slowly, as if invisible hands were guiding her down. And she could move her arms and legs. She placed her fingers across her face as she opened her eyes, peeking between them to see what was around her as she continued to fall.

Books surrounded her, stacked and stuffed on shelves on every side. Because she was moving so slowly, she could reach out for one, clasping on to the paperback and pulling it close to her. She stared at the cover and gasped: it was a drawing of her with the title *The Life of Ella Finn*. She was going to open it when it snapped out of her hand like a rubber band and flew back to where she'd got it.

Then she hit the ground with a thump. Her ribs ached as she rolled to the side to see Jack peering at her.

'Come on, Ella, get a move on.'

She sat up and pulled her legs towards her with arms placed over her knees.

'No. I'm not moving until you tell me what's going on.'

He removed an apple from his pocket and offered it to her. She was about to shake her head until her stomach grumbled; she couldn't remember the last time she'd eaten. Ella grabbed it and took a large bite, crunching it between her teeth.

'What do you mean, Ella?'

'Those big eyes in the sky earlier, you said that was me. Explain that to me.'

Jack sat next to her and took a small cloth from his pocket. He unfolded it and placed it in front of them.

'Okay, but I need to eat as well.' He dipped into his

pocket and removed two packs of sandwiches. 'Cheese and onion for both of us. I hope you like them.'

She didn't complain, putting what was left of the apple down and grabbing the food. She'd eaten half of one as she spoke.

'How come you have so much stuff in your jacket?'

He grinned at her. 'Do you remember what I said about Everywhere being connected to every realm in existence?' Ella nodded as she bit through a large piece of onion. 'Well, some items, and people, are also linked to other realms.' He patted the jacket. 'These pockets are linked to the greatest kitchens in the multiverse. And that means I'll never starve.'

She finished a sandwich and started on the other. 'Did Pandora create all of this?'

'I doubt it. No one knows who created the multiverse, but plenty claim to be gods who can create life. I don't know what this Pandora has or hasn't done, but she didn't create all the different realms.' He moved closer to Ella. 'Understand that everything exists somewhere. All the things you believed to be imaginary in your world are real somewhere else. What you've read in books or seen in movies exists somewhere in Everywhere.'

'As we were falling, I saw a book with my face on it which was about my life. What was that?'

'You glimpsed another realm, where you only exist in someone's mind.'

Ella spat a piece of cheese on to the ground.

'I don't exist?'

Jack laughed. 'Of course you exist. But in some realms, you're only a figment of somebody's imagination. A person dreamt about you and then created a story about your life. They probably tapped into Everywhere and saw you.'

The thought made Ella's head hurt.

'Does that mean in some other realm, people might read about us in a book? Read about us talking like this?'

He dipped into his pocket and removed a bottle of water. He offered it to her.

'Perhaps. Or maybe they're watching us in a movie or a TV show.'

'Cool.' She ran her fingers through her hair and hoped she didn't look like a scarecrow. 'How do you know about TV shows and movies?'

'Oh, I know all kinds of things, Ella, about your world and many others.' He patted her knee. 'I'm older than I look and well-travelled.'

She drank from the bottle. The water tasted of strawberries.

'So, you've met me in the future?'

He nodded. 'Yes.'

'That means you know what will happen to us on this journey.'

He shook his head. 'No. When I met you, it was the end for you, but the beginning for me. In the multiverse, as you call it, there are many versions of all of us. The other you I met might not be this you at all. Does that make sense?'

'No.' She rubbed at her eyes. 'My brain hurts. What did the future me tell you?'

'Just to go with you.'

'Why did you?'

Jack shrugged. 'Life is boring without an adventure, don't you think?'

Ella didn't know what to think anymore. She stood.

'I need to find Pandora.'

He stood as well. 'And then what? How will you prevent her returning to your world and ruling it?'

Ella glanced at her hands. 'Pandora has power, but

because I'm related to her, so do I. That's how I could follow her. I'll use that to stop her, or I'll gather an army to fight her.'

'Do you still have this power?'

She stared at her palms. 'I don't know. Not at this moment anyway.' She looked around her. 'But I think I'm still connected to her. I can feel her close by.'

He took the bottle from her and returned it to his jacket.

'Then we'd better get a move on.'

They walked together through a landscape of pretty flowers, bursting with all the colours of the rainbow and smelling so sweet, she thought she'd pass out from a sugar rush. Ella wanted to ask him more questions, but kept them for later. Her head still hurt from what he'd said.

There are different versions of me out there, in this multiverse. That's what that book must have been about. I wish I could have kept it. It might have told me how to defeat Pandora.

She'd left home to gather knowledge about Pandora and maybe an army, but she still wasn't sure how to do the second part. Why would soldiers or warriors help her in a battle with Pandora? She didn't even have money to pay them.

Ella was considering this problem when she heard sounds up ahead. She thought she recognised the tune, and as they got closer, she realised it was *Wrecking Ball* by Miley Cyrus. She knew little about pop music, but she couldn't forget that one as all the kids at school had been singing it a few years ago.

She glanced at Jack as the music stopped. Then a blood-curdling scream shattered the silence and he reached out for her arm.

'Are you good at fighting?'

Ella scrunched up her nose at him. 'It depends on what I have to fight.'

They strode into an open area and saw many penguins standing around, speaking in a language she didn't understand. They were all wearing top hats, and the biggest one in the middle held a silver cane.

It turned to them.

'Welcome, little girl and Mr Rabbit. Are you here for the Dance Party Challenge?'

She moved forward, enchanted by the smiles greeting them. She held out her hand.

'I'm Ella and my friend is Jack. But I don't know how to dance.'

The big penguin with the cane took her hand in its wing and shook her fingers so hard, she thought her arm might drop off.

'I'm Queen Amanda, and this is my dance troupe.' She let go of Ella and grinned at her. 'What do you mean, child, that you can't dance? Every living thing has the Rhythm inside them.'

Ella's cheeks warmed and she knew her face was turning pink.

'I tried to dance at the school disco last year, but my feet got all tangled, and I fell on my face just as the music stopped. Everyone laughed at me, including some teachers.' She glanced at Jack. 'I've always been clumsy.'

Queen Armada threw a large wing around Ella and pulled her towards the other penguins.

'You were young then, child. Now you're growing up, and the Rhythm is rising and changing you. Do you know what the Rhythm is?'

Ella thought she did. 'Movement to sounds or music?'

The Queen let go of her. 'Yes, in a primitive sense, that's

what it is.' She pressed her wing against her chest. 'But deep in here, the Rhythm gives all living things strength and life. The more you have, the stronger you become.' She looked at the other penguins. 'And we're the strongest of all.' Then she stared at Jack. 'So which of you is here to take the challenge?'

Jack stepped forward. 'Begging your pardon, Queen Amanda, but we are just travellers searching for our friend.' He showed the Queen the photos on his phone. 'Have you seen her?'

The penguin blinked twice. 'Yes. She's powerful with the Rhythm, that one.'

'When was she here?' Ella said.

The Queen twirled the stick with her wing.

'It might have been tomorrow or yesterday. I'm always confused by time.'

Ella furrowed her brow. 'Was it recently?'

Amanda stopped fiddling with the cane and peered at her.

'It was about an hour ago. She was an excellent dancer. One of the few winners we've had here in a long time.' She snapped her head towards Ella. 'So, are you ready for the challenge?'

Ella smiled at her. 'As my friend said, we're only travelling. And I can't dance.'

The other penguins moved forward into a line alongside their Queen.

'You need to dance and win to get past us. That is the toll you must pay. No dancing means no progress.'

Jack pulled Ella towards him. 'Let's try another route. It's not worth the trouble.'

Ella stared at the wall of penguins. 'But we know

Pandora went this way. We have to follow, or I might never find her. And I'm sure you can dance.'

He let go of her. 'Oh no, I have two left feet. It has to be you, Ella.'

She sighed loudly. 'Okay. What's the worst that might happen?'

Queen Amanda stepped towards her. 'If you lose, you pay the price.'

'What price?' Ella said.

All the penguins rubbed their bellies as their leader spoke.

'We eat you. Penguins can't live on fish alone, you know.' She licked her lips. 'And it's such a long time since we've dined on a human.'

The birds separated and Ella saw something piled up behind them. She didn't know what it was at first until the sunlight reflected off the pile and she realised it was bones.

3 LOST IN MUSIC

Invisible fingers clutched at her heart as Jack grabbed her again.

'Let's find another path, Ella.'

But there was no other way, and she knew it.

The penguins continued to rub at their bellies as they opened their mouths and showed her six sets of giant fangs. Music played out of nowhere, and the birds started tap dancing, moving their feet up and down as their teeth grew over their lips while they glared at her.

Ella was transfixed as Jack spoke in her ear.

'I hate this song.' She shook her head, not knowing what it was. 'It's *Bohemian Rhapsody*.'

The penguins appeared to love it, gnashing and swaying as they sang along with the lyrics. Queen Amanda broke away from the others, spinning towards Ella as she twirled the cane above her. Behind them, the pile of bones sparkled in the sun. Ella pulled at the collar of her shirt as the sweat trickled down her forehead.

How am I going to dance against these and win?

Jack must have read her thoughts. 'If we run now while they're dancing, we might get away.'

But where would they go, and how would they find Pandora? They were already at least an hour behind her.

The volume increased and Ella tried to make out where the melody was coming from, but she saw no band or music player. It just appeared from thin air and hovered every-where. Perhaps this was the land of free tunes. She ignored the music as she watched the penguins going through their routine, amazed at the way they swivelled and shimmied in sequence without putting a foot wrong. She'd seen a film about dancing penguins, but this was on another level.

Their movements mesmerised her, but it was mainly all those teeth chewing up and down that held her attention. Thankfully they'd stopped growing, but she knew any one of the penguins could swallow her whole.

The routine ended with a flourish, the other five penguins grabbing Queen Amanda and throwing her into the air, where she twisted twice before landing like a super-hero with the cane held above her head.

Then the music ended as suddenly as it had started.

The Queen grinned at Ella through those vast teeth.

'Now, child, you must choose which of us to battle in the dance and pick your tune.'

'I know nothing about music.' She'd watched the other kids at school singing to stuff on their phones or dancing to videos on YouTube, but nothing had grabbed at her the way it did them. She couldn't think of any tune to help move her clumsy feet. She stalled for time as she racked her brain. 'I only dance against one of you?'

The Queen nodded. 'That's correct.' She pointed at the penguin on the end. 'Sarah is the least experienced, so you might have a slight chance against her.'

'If I choose you and win, we get safe passage through, and if I lose, you get to eat us both?'

Jack groaned as the Queen licked her lips.

'That's right, child.'

Ella smiled at her. 'But I need more than that.'

The Queen blinked. 'What do you want?'

'Information. I want you to tell me what you know about the woman who came through before us. Her name is Pandora.'

'Why should I do that?'

'If I win the dance, will you answer my questions?'

Amanda's laugh was loud and the other penguins joined her.

'Child, if you can beat me, I'll tell you anything you want.'

Jack grabbed Ella and pulled her from the Queen.

'Are you mad?' He nipped her skin and she wriggled from his grip. 'This whole thing is crazy, but at least pick the weakest of them, not her.'

'I know what I'm doing, Jack. Don't you trust me?'

His paw trembled as he dipped into his pocket. He removed a bottle of green liquid and took a large gulp from it. Ella didn't know what it was, but she caught a whiff of it, which smelt of cough medicine.

'I guess I do, Ella.'

The Queen's voice boomed over them.

'I accept your challenge, Ella Finn. What tune will we do battle to?'

Ella still hadn't thought of one. What could she pick that might match up to her clumsy feet and legs? The Queen was lurching forward, cane swinging next to her when the song came to her. It was her mother's favourite, the tune she sang in the morning before taking Ella to school.

How could I forget it?

Before she could tell Queen Amanda the name, the first bars appeared from nowhere, as if someone had read her mind.

'Who decides the winner?' Ella said over the intro.

The Queen grinned at her through huge teeth.

'Why, I do, of course. My game means it's my rules.'

Ella scowled at her. 'That's not fair.'

Amanda lifted the cane above her head and the music stopped, paused on one beat which kept on repeating.

'Fair! Nothing in life is fair. Haven't you learnt that yet? How old are you, five?'

Ella was two days away from her thirteenth birthday when she'd left home and stepped into Everywhere, but she knew that time moved differently here.

I bet I missed my birthday.

'I'm thirteen,' she said.

'Well, thirteen-year-old Ella, you're about to get a lesson in how harsh life is.'

The Queen twirled the cane in the air and the music burst around them. She went straight into an extravagant dance routine, twirling the stick along one wing, and then spinning it over the back of her neck and down the other side. As she did that, her feet twitched from side to side in a frenzy, shuffling across the ground at dizzying speed.

Ella's head hurt as she watched her opponent until she shook the sight from her brain and remembered her mother swivelling her hips and singing at the top of her voice as she grabbed Ella's hands and danced around the kitchen. She'd lead Ella out of the kitchen, through the corridor and into the living room as they boogied between the furniture and avoided the books and magazines her parents had stacked on the floor.

Ella remembered it all, moving to avoid tables and chairs, piles of papers and the cat dashing between them. Now her body resurrected the moves as her feet sprang to life, injecting energy she'd never felt before into her legs and hips.

She jumped a foot into the air, expecting to hurtle back down with a crash, but she hung there like a puppet; yet no one was controlling Ella but her. Queen Amanda stopped dancing, her teeth shrinking into her mouth as she gawped at Ella.

'Crikey Mikey,' Jack said.

All the penguins gazed at Ella open-mouthed.

Then Ella rose another foot and danced on air, swaying her hips and waving her hands above her head. There was no rhyme or reason for what she did, her body moving as if it was the most natural thing in the world. The lyrics fell from her lips as she pirouetted between a group of birds who stared at her through dazed eyes.

As the music surged through every inch of her, Ella did two quick somersaults and a backflip. For a moment, she couldn't see the birds or Jack, only her mother dancing around the house. She could smell her mother's perfume, all rosewater and lavender, and hear her voice singing in her mind.

It only disappeared with the sound of clapping from below. Ella twisted her head to peer at the penguins and Jack cheering her. Queen Amanda was banging her cane in the dirt before bowing to Ella.

Ella stopped dancing on air, waiting to crash to the ground, surprised when she floated back to earth. Amanda stepped forward and bowed again. Then all the other penguins followed suit.

Jack ran to her. 'Are you okay?'

Her heart thumped against her chest and electricity surged through her legs, but she felt fine. In fact, she'd never felt better.

'I'm great, Jack.'

He did his own little jig on the spot.

'How did you do that?' He pointed to the sky. 'Flying around and everything.'

Ella shook her head. 'I don't know.'

The Queen approached them.

'You are the clear winner, Ella Finn, so the Penguins of the Dance offer you safe passage through here.'

Ella thanked her. 'And now you'll answer my questions?'

Amanda nodded. 'If I can.'

'Tell me what happened when Pandora took your challenge.'

The Queen gripped the top of her cane.

'She danced against three of us, moving to the sounds of *Vogue* by Madonna.'

A strange thought struck Ella. 'Do you always dance to music from other worlds?'

'Sometimes,' Queen Amanda said. 'But you humans have all the best tunes.'

Ella grinned before remembering what she wanted to know.

'And Pandora was a better dancer than your group?'

'The Rhythm flowed through her like a river. My penguins were shattered after the contest.'

'I need to find warriors to help me fight her. Have you had any others come through here who could do that?'

'Only one,' Amanda replied.

Ella's heart shrank. One. What could one person do against Pandora?

'What's their name?' Ella said.

The Queen laughed like a thunderclap.

'Her name is Ella.'

She kept on laughing as she rolled the cane over her wing and returned to the other penguins.

'See,' Jack said. 'You're the one to defeat Pandora.'

Ella watched the strange birds leave.

'Maybe. We won't know until we find her, and she has a head start.'

Ella strode in the opposite direction to the one they'd come from, with Jack by her side.

'What you did was magnificent, Ella, but what was the music you danced to?'

Ella thought of her mother again and what she had to do to save her and everyone else on Earth.

'It was *Dancing Queen.*'

4 TIME AFTER TIME

They left the penguins behind and entered a garden filled with large flowering trees. Ella's father had been a keen gardener before he'd disappeared and then reappeared, and she'd enjoyed helping him in the garden at the back of their house. He'd taught her something about - what did he call it? Haughty something - and she'd started a collection of buds and leaves before her parents had vanished.

She considered herself to be quite knowledgeable for a girl of twelve, probably now thirteen, but she recognised nothing growing in this garden apart from the grass they strode across. And even that looked a little different to her.

Ella let Jack go on ahead as she bent and ran her fingers through the field, surprised the blades felt like wool. And as she pushed her head closer, she took a deep breath and realised they smelt like fresh custard.

'What are you doing, Ella?' Jack stood over her. She ignored him and lay on her back over the custard grass, staring into the marshmallow-coloured sky. 'I thought you were in a rush.'

Ella reached into her pocket and removed the phone. She pointed the screen at him.

'I was until I saw this.'

He stared at it for one minute. 'The clock isn't moving.' She sat up and looked at him. 'That's because time moves differently in some of these places compared to your world, Ella. We might go somewhere and you'll age twenty years in a day.'

Ella grabbed at her face and wondered if she'd look like her mother as she got older. Then she told him how she'd found the Book of All Life inside the secret house on the clifftop.

'And in the house, time moved differently to outside, but I discovered it was the same as in the place Pandora came from. This meant thirty minutes in her world was four hours in mine. So I tricked her into going away and not returning for five years. Five years in her world means forty in mine.'

Jack nodded. 'That was clever, to give you more time in designing a plan to deal with her.'

'Yes, but then I followed her through the gateway, and if I'm here too long, when I get back..., when I get back...'

She couldn't finish the sentence.

'You think you'll still be young like you are now, and your family and friends will have aged a lot?'

She clutched at her chest. 'Won't they?'

Jack shrugged. 'I don't know, Ella. Like I said, time flows differently from place to place.'

'Do you know how to get to my world from here?'

He glanced around their surroundings.

'I don't. Do you?'

She shook her head and stared at the unmoving clock on her phone.

'So, I don't know where Pandora is or what I'll do when I find her, and if I'm still alive when this is all over, everyone I know might be fifty years older when I get home. If I can find my home.'

Jack handed her a bar of chocolate, her favourite with toffee in the middle of it. 'How do you know I like this?'

'Don't all children like chocolate?'

'Yes, but how do you know this is my favourite?' She ripped the paper from the top of it. 'Oh wait, let me guess: that big head in the sky which is a future me or a different me told you, didn't it?'

He shrugged. 'You are very clever, Ella Finn.'

She bit into the bar and tasted the delicious chocolate as it melted in her mouth. Ella peered into the clouds and wondered if perhaps they should rest before going after Pandora. The grass where she sat was more comfortable than a soft bed. The sun was shining, and with Jack's multiverse jacket, they'd never go hungry or thirsty. And the clock still hadn't moved on her phone, so maybe she had all the time in the world.

Time to make a plan for Pandora.

She hadn't thought of a plan when she'd stepped into the place Jack called Everywhere, rushing through without a care about what she'd do when she caught up with Pandora.

Now would be a good time to think of one.

That crossed her mind as she noticed small, dark shadows creeping towards them. She should have jumped up with a start, but all she could do was smile. She tried to say something to Jack, but the words came out of her lips in slow motion.

'We've...'

'Got...'

'Company.'

'You've got trouble; that's what you've got.'

Her eyelids were like lead and just about to close when the talking cat threw a net over her head.

ELLA WOKE up in a cage sometime later. A thousand tiny fists punched the back of her skull as she opened her eyes and peered at Jack in the cage opposite.

Ella rubbed her neck. 'What happened?'

He pushed his head against the bars of his prison.

'There was something in the grass which made us drowsy. Or maybe it was those strange flowers in the trees. Whatever it was, it left us as no match when the cats arrived.'

She remembered the voice and the net draped over her head.

'The cats?'

Jack's face trembled as he spoke.

'I hate cats.'

Ella licked the inside of her mouth, which was as dry as sand.

'I like them.' She twisted her back in the small place that imprisoned her. 'Do all animals talk in this multiverse?'

He squinted at her. 'Yes. Why wouldn't they?'

'Animals can't talk in my world.'

He shivered again. 'That must be terrible, not to have a voice. How do they communicate with humans?'

'They don't.'

His strange eyes glazed over.

'So how do they live their lives?'

Ella didn't know what to tell him.

'I thought you'd been to my world, to Earth. You speak English and know things about us, like music.' She scratched at a spot on her neck. 'In fact, you and these cats and the snarks and the penguins can all speak English. How is that possible?'

He shrugged. 'Some things are universal across the different realms, and other times things seep from one world into others. These are shared over the worlds.'

She pushed her back into the bars behind her.

'So what do these cats want with us?'

Everything she'd met so far, apart from Jack, had wanted to eat her, so she waited for him to give her the bad news.

'I'm afraid it's my fault, Ella. I didn't expect the cats to be here; otherwise, I'd have been on my guard.'

'Why is it your fault?'

He pushed his arms through the bars.

'It's because of this jacket. They want it back.'

Before she could reply, a group of moggies marched into the room carrying small spears. One of them stepped forward, his ginger fur glistening in the light creeping through the window.

'Prisoners, it's time for your trial.' He pointed his spear at his comrades. 'Bring them to the court.'

Ella was wondering how the felines, who were just normal-sized cats, would carry them out when they pushed their spears into holes at the cages' bottom. Only when they moved forward did she realise their prisons were on wheels. The cats rolled them side by side so she could talk to Jack.

'What's this got to do with your jacket?'

He was so close to her, he could pass a banana across. Jack ate a carrot as she peeled her fruit.

'I might have taken it from them a while back.'

'What do you mean, taken it from them?'

'I won it in a bet, and they're not happy about it.'

'You lie,' the main cat said as he rattled Jack's cage with his spear. 'You stole the Magic Jacket from us.'

Jack leant close so he could whisper to her.

'They don't know about the multiverse and believe what I wear is magical.'

'Why don't they just take it from you and let us go?'

He shook his head as they got outside.

'They can't. It's all part of their culture. Once I've put it on, they can only have it if I give it to them willingly.'

'So why don't you?'

He didn't answer as the cats pulled them into the middle of a vast square. As she peered through the bars, Ella saw they were in an arena surrounded by high walls and what seemed like hundreds of cats glaring at them. A large tabby strode forward and addressed the crowd.

'The Thief and his accomplice will now face feline justice and the sentence of this court.'

'Give it back to them, Jack. Then we can leave.'

'I can't, Ella.'

Before she replied, the tabby spoke again.

'What do you say, my fellow felines? Are they innocent or guilty?'

A large combined meow hummed around the arena before turning into one repeated word.

'Guilty. Guilty. Guilty.'

It continued for a minute before the tabby raised her paw and a hush settled over them.

'Guilty it is, and the sentence is death.'

Ella's blood was boiling when she decided she'd had enough. She flexed her arms and stretched her back up and into the top of the cage. The flimsy wood snapped quickly, and she stood up straight. Her body ached as hundreds of angry cats hissed at her.

'Kill the witch, kill the witch,' they shouted.

She ignored their cries and stepped towards Jack's prison. She reached down and tore the front apart. He rolled out, and then stood next to her.

'Kill the witch, kill the witch,' they cried with their strange cat voices.

Ella had had enough and stamped her foot so hard, dust flew into the air in great clouds.

'I'm not a witch.'

The tabby crept towards her. 'We know what you are, girl. You sent your familiar, that rabbit here, to steal our Magic Jacket, all the while knowing it was our only means of food. Do you know how many have died since he stole it?'

Pain shot through her heart. 'You have no food?'

'Not enough to feed us all. One of your kind, another human, fed on our land and turned it barren, so there's nothing left but the Dream Flowers, and too many of those will kill you.'

Ella went to Jack. 'Give me your mobile.' He did without argument. She found the photos of Pandora and showed them to the cat. 'Is this her?'

She hissed at the image. 'You know it is.'

'When did she do this?'

The tabby glared at her. 'Three days ago, one week after your familiar stole what was ours.'

Ella thrust the phone back at the rabbit.

'Give them the jacket, Jack.'

He sighed heavily. 'I wish I could, Ella, but it won't come off.'

'What do you mean?'

'I've tried to remove it, I have, but it won't come off. Watch if you don't believe me.'

He put his paws on either side at the front and tried to pull it from his body, but it wouldn't budge. So she tried the same, and it wouldn't move for her, either.

'Is it magic?' she said to him.

Jack shook his head. 'I don't know, Ella.'

The ginger cat moved towards them.

'Didn't you wonder, foolish creature, why we had it hanging on the wall in the grand palace? Great magic flows through it, too much for any living thing to come into contact with it for too long without suffering dire consequences. As you have now discovered.'

Ella addressed the cat. 'He'll return the jacket to you. Just tell us how to get it off him.'

The cat laughed. 'Why, that's easy. All he has to do is die and it will fall right off his corpse.'

Ella puffed out her cheeks.

'Great.'

5 THE LOVE CATS

The tabby smiled at her. 'I have your permission to kill the familiar?'

'No, you don't. And he's not a familiar. And I'm not a witch. I'll sort this out for you without killing him.'

The cat peered at her through curious eyes.

'How will you do that if you're not a witch?'

It was a good question for which she didn't have an answer. Yet.

'First things first. What's your name?'

'I'm Lucy, the Grand Chancellor of this community.'

'Well, in these unusual circumstances, it's nice to meet you and your people, Lucy.' Ella turned to the rabbit. 'Dig deep into your pockets and feed everyone here, Jack.'

'Okay, Ella. That's going to keep me busy for a while. What will you be doing while I'm doing that?'

She stared at the crowd of cats surrounding them.

'Trying to keep you alive, my new friend.'

Lucy led them back inside, not caged this time, through a different entrance. They followed her down a long dusty corridor until they entered a large hall. The place was empty, apart from a few bowls of rotting vegetables and dirty water.

'That's all we have left now.' The moggy bowed her head. 'Only that for two hundred and sixty-four of us.'

Ella nodded at Jack while she sat next to Lucy. The rabbit dipped into both pockets of his jacket and removed a succession of food and water. Her mind raced through how to deal with Pandora as she watched cat after cat enter the hall while Jack gave them refreshments.

The time on her phone still hadn't moved, so she didn't know how long she sat like that, but he must have fed a hundred cats before he stopped and came to her.

'You need food and drink, Ella.' She didn't argue as the hole in her stomach pressed against her ribs. 'What would you like?'

She replied immediately. 'A veggie burger with fries.'

Jack grinned as he reached into his pocket and removed what she'd requested. She grabbed it from him and bit into the burger so hard, tomato sauce dribbled over her lips. He sat and watched her, nibbling on a carrot as he did. Ella ate half of the food before speaking.

'Your jacket doesn't reach into a kitchen somewhere in the multiverse, does it?'

He shook his head. 'No, it doesn't. All I have to do is think of what food or drink I want, and it appears in a pocket.'

She wiped at her mouth. 'I guess it's magical after all.' She drank from the bottle of water he'd given her. 'Is that why you stole it? So you'd never go hungry or thirsty again?'

Jack finished his carrot and laughed.

'Not quite. I was misinformed about the true nature of this jacket.'

'How so?'

'Someone told me the pockets were full of treasure that never ended.'

'And you thought that meant gold and jewels?'

He shrugged. 'Wouldn't you?'

She glanced around the hall at the cats eating and drinking.

'This is a real treasure, Jack. You took something which keeps hundreds, if not thousands, alive just for yourself. Why would you do that?'

For the first time since she'd met him, she saw defiance in his eyes.

'I'm a thief. That's what we do.'

He stood and left her, going to feed the rest of the cats. That's when she realised she didn't know him at all. It made her think of Pandora when she was Dora and they'd become friends. She'd trusted her, and look how that turned out.

That's why I'm here now.

She finished her food as Lucy approached.

'Would you like to see what Pandora did to us?'

Ella nodded, and then stood. Lucy led her through the hall and past the happy cats out through the back door. Fresh air filled her lungs and she was glad to be outside again. That was until she glanced into the horizon and saw the devastation.

Lucy lifted a paw and pointed to the vast space on the right.

'That was the lake where we got our drinking water.' Then she pointed to the black earth next to it. 'And that was where the crops grew every year without fail.'

Ella took a deep breath. 'What did Pandora do?'

'I witnessed it all,' Lucy said. 'That woman staggered into our community as if she was at death's door. Her face was all haggard, with bloodshot eyes and withered skin. I was about to run and help her when she threw herself into the lake. I and a few others raced towards her, fearful she might drown. We don't get many outsiders here, but the occasional traveller passes through to tell us tales of other worlds. I knew she'd die if we didn't get to her soon. Yet, just as we reached the edge, something terrible happened.'

Ella could see it in her head. 'All the water drained from the lake.'

The cat nodded. 'Yes. All that was left was the woman standing there with a great grin on her face. Then, before we could say or do anything, she went to the crops and thrust her arms into the ground.'

Ella stared across at the scorched earth. 'And she sucked the life from the soil?'

Lucy wiped a tear from her eye. 'And now nothing will grow there, with no rain even though this is the rainy season.' She stared at Ella. 'Do you know what this woman did to our land?'

Ella thought she did. 'I noticed in the great hall that your community only eats vegetables. Don't you ever eat meat?'

Lucy laughed. 'What meat would we eat? Apart from the odd traveller, we're the only living things here. And we wouldn't eat each other, would we?'

Ella glanced into the sky. 'There are no birds here?'

'A few, but nobody eats birds.' Lucy narrowed her eyes at Ella. 'Do they eat birds in your world?'

'Unfortunately, yes.' She didn't have the heart to tell her the rest, peering into the dead earth instead. She'd worked enough times in the garden with her dad to know how things grew in the ground. 'Do you plant seeds for your crops?'

Lucy shook her head. 'We do nothing. For as long as

we've been here, the crops have grown, we've removed them, and then they've grown again. It happens all year round, year after year.'

Ella strode down the hill and stopped at the edge of the barren ground. It smelt of rotten food, which got worse as she knelt and touched the soil. It was cold to the touch, and she knew what Pandora had done.

She drained them of their Light.

That essence gave everything life, what Jack called the Glow and her parents said was the human soul. Pandora said it was Light, and she'd taken it from the land and the lake.

But why?

'The community has spoken about leaving here.' Lucy stood at her side. 'But we wouldn't know where to go. We've lived here all our lives, just like our parents and their ancestors before them, stretching back centuries.'

Ella smiled. 'You won't have to leave.'

She knew what she had to do, but wasn't sure it would work.

But I have to try.

Because she was descended from Pandora, so Pandora claimed, Ella had the same powers as her, only her Light wasn't fully developed because she was too young. But she didn't feel young now, in this strange land, this Everywhere. She stared into her palms, knowing she was different.

Perhaps I'm all grown up.

Perhaps it was because there were other versions of her connected to this place, and all of them lived through her.

Ella thought about that as she leant over and pushed her fingers into the dead earth. She closed her eyes and remembered how the Light had flowed from Pandora to her back home. She knew it was still there, the spark that had made her fly and dance in the air above the penguins.

The stench of death jumped from the earth and into her mouth, thrusting down into her lungs and grabbing at her heart. She pushed her hands further into the ground, feeling the dry dirt crumbling between her fingers.

Then Ella reached into her mind and found that moment she'd had with Pandora, grabbing on to the Light lurking at the bottom of who she was. Her hands twitched as she dragged the Light up, enjoying the warmth as it ran through her blood and bones. When it reached the top of her, she let it go, and it seeped from her skin and into the black soil.

She thought she sat there for an eternity, listening to *Dancing Queen* on a loop inside her head. When it finally stopped, she opened her eyes and saw Pandora grinning at her.

Then Ella passed out.

JACK HAD her hand in his paw when she woke. There was an emptiness in her stomach that was bigger than the worst hunger she'd ever felt. Like the rest of her, her eyes were tired, and she rubbed at them, hardly believing what was in front of her.

Hundreds of cats stood on their hind legs, swaying from side to side as they let out a long combined meow. Then, as Jack helped her up, the cats parted and turned to look at her as she saw the most fantastic thing. What had once been dead earth, a massive expanse of blackened soil, was packed with crops standing six feet tall. They swayed in the wind and mirrored the rhythm of the felines.

As Jack squeezed her hand, she got a sudden rush of an aroma of freshwater filling her head. It made her dizzy, and she grabbed hold of him to steady herself.

'It worked, then,' she said.

Lucy lifted a paw and pointed at what had once been the empty lake.

'This is far better than it was. The crops are bigger and more numerous than before. And look.'

Now, it was full of water, and even from where she was, Ella could see the fish jumping in the middle of it.

Ella stared into her hands. 'I'm tired, but I feel good.'

'So you should, Ella Finn,' Lucy said. 'You saved us all.'

The tabby threw her paws into the air and danced a jig on two legs while all the other cats followed her example.

'Are you hungry?' Jack said.

Ella gazed at the fish leaping out of the lake, feeling guilty she'd somehow brought them there to be eaten by the cats. She tried not to think about it as she rubbed at her belly.

'I'm starving. What have you got?'

He grinned at her and put both paws in his pockets.

'Whatever you want. Does this mean I get to keep this jacket?'

She thought about it for two seconds, imagining what would happen to this community of cats if they lost their crops and lake again.

'No. Lucy and the others still need it for emergencies.'

He furrowed his eyebrows at her.

'So what happens now?'

Ella grinned at him.

'I have to kill you, Jack.'

6 SONG OF THE FACTORY

Ella had given the whole thing careful thought, even before she'd resurrected the water and the land, but her little fainting session had confirmed her plan. But it didn't convince Jack when she explained it to him.

'Are you sure about this?' He stood hunched over a foul-smelling liquid brew.

'Don't you trust me?'

He straightened his back and stared at her.

'Let me go over this again.' He pulled at his collar. 'This magical piece of clothing will only come off me when I'm dead.' He glanced at the group of cats peering at him from the corner. 'So you want to use a concoction of those flowers which made us dizzy earlier to knock me out and trick it into thinking I'm dead. Is that right?'

She moved towards him. 'You don't like this plan?'

He rubbed at his chin. 'No, not really, but, well, what's the worst that can happen once I've drunk this devilish liquid? I'll have a sore head and the jacket.'

Lucy jumped up on to the table.

'Or you'll be dead and we'll have it back.'

Jack looked at Ella. 'Are you sure?'

'I am.'

She'd explained to him the importance of the jacket if the crops failed again and understood this was only his nerves speaking. He took a deep breath and reached for the bowl. He hesitated for a second before drinking the whole thing in one go. Then he returned the dish to the table and wiped his arm across his mouth.

'Actually, it didn't taste that bad.'

Then she watched as his eyes glazed over before he collapsed.

HE WOKE TEN MINUTES LATER.

'How do you feel?' Ella said.

Jack touched his head. 'As if the world has fallen on me.'

She smiled. 'Which world?'

He sat up and reached for his pockets, digging his paws inside and finding them empty.

'It worked, then?'

She nodded. 'I whipped the jacket off you, and the cats provided you with a new one.'

He exhaled. 'Let's get out of here.'

'I've got something for you before you leave,' Lucy said as she approached them. 'We can never repay you for what you've done, but I'd like to help you on your quest.'

'Our quest?' Ella said.

'To defeat this Pandora. If you don't find an army, you'll need something better.'

'What's that?' Jack said.

'Information. Knowledge. The more you learn about her, the better equipped you'll be to overthrow her.'

Ella knew the cat was right.

'Do you have this information, Lucy?'

Lucy shook her tiny head.

'Unfortunately, I don't. But I know where you can find the one who does.'

'Who is it?' Ella said.

'When you leave here, go north beyond the lake. That's where Pandora went. On your way, you'll reach the Kingdom, and in there is the one you want. He's called Merlin.'

'Merlin? The wizard?'

Lucy shrugged. 'I don't know. All I know are the legends of Everywhere claiming Merlin as the font of all knowledge. If anyone knows how to defeat Pandora, it will be Merlin.'

Ella thanked Lucy and the rest of the felines as they gave her and Jack a bag full of provisions for the journey. As she left the hall, she glanced at the far end where the magical jacket hung on the wall.

Nearly three hundred cats standing on their hind legs and shaking their paws waved them on their way. Jack pulled at the sleeves of his new coat as they strode past the lake.

'I feel naked without the other one.'

She laughed at him. 'You'll get used to it, my friend. Clothes aren't important. It's who's inside them that counts.'

They talked as they walked, with him speaking first.

'Do you believe Pandora left your world because you tricked her or for some other reason?'

'What other reason?'

She didn't like to think he was questioning her skills as a trickster.

'Well, you told me you'd absorbed some of her Light.'

'Did I?'

She couldn't remember telling him that, but Ella found the more time she spent in this strange place, the more confusing it became.

'Yes, and isn't that what you used to bring life back to the crops and that lake?'

'I suppose so.' She considered his words. 'Are you saying she ran from my world because she was weak, and that's why she drained what she could from the cat community?'

'Don't you think so?'

'I guess it's possible.'

'Which means, if she's weakened, you could deal with her on your own, without an army or any warriors.'

'I suppose so.'

Though she still didn't know what she'd do to contain Pandora. She couldn't kill her.

I'm not a murderer.

'I think that's why she's running back to wherever her home is,' Jack said.

'We can ask Merlin when we find him.'

She knew all about Merlin and the legends of Camelot from books she'd read.

Perhaps I'll meet King Arthur and the Knights of the Round Table with Merlin.

After walking for twenty minutes, they came to a large wood. As they entered it, Ella waited for the sounds of woodland creatures, of the birds and smaller animals, but it was so quiet, she could have heard a pin drop. They kept going for half a minute before she recognised a familiar aroma.

Jack stopped and wiggled his nose.

'What is that stink?'

She glanced up between the branches, searching for smoke, but there was nothing but clear blue sky there. Ella knew the smell from the factories near where she used to play.

'It's chemicals.'

They moved forward, stepping past the trees and into a clearing. Beyond them, reaching up into the clouds, she saw the chimney stacks spewing out their foul pollution. But it wasn't those which surprised her.

There were rows of giant mushrooms about two hundred yards ahead. Things were sitting on top of each mushroom, but she couldn't see what they were from where they stood.

Jack came up to her.

'Should we try going around this?'

Ella shook her head. 'Let's get closer to see what they are first.'

They moved ahead, staying cautious in case anybody was watching them.

'My, my,' Jack said as they saw what was sitting on each mushroom.

Ella put a hand to her face.

'Babies!'

She rubbed her eyes in case she was dreaming. But she wasn't. A baby sat atop each mushroom, close enough to the edge that one slip would send them tumbling to the ground.

'What do we do, Ella?'

She didn't know, but as she tried to think of an answer, a vast screech cut through the air. They put their hands over their ears as Ella peered at the tremendous pink bird swooping down and snatching a baby with its beak.

'It grabbed the baby's clothes.'

'What was that?'

'A stork.' She'd seen pictures of them in books at school.

As they stood there gaping in surprise, the screeching came again, this time from dozens of the birds. They flew down in bunches, pink and blue ones, and picked up a baby from each mushroom. It took less than a minute for every child to be gone, and Ella got another hit of that chemical stink.

'Were those human babies, Ella?'

She nodded. 'They were.'

'Is that how humans reproduce?'

Heat spread through her cheeks. She'd had the classes and her mother had spoken to her about where babies came from. Some girls at school thought you got them from the shops like shoes or toys, but she knew it didn't happen like that, or like this.

'Not at home, but perhaps it is in this world.'

'Why were the birds different colours?' he said.

Ella scratched at her chin. 'Pink for girls and blue for boys.'

Jack narrowed his eyes. 'Why?'

She shrugged. 'I don't know.'

They continued moving, heading for whatever was spewing smoke into the air. Despite her adventures so far, exciting as they'd been, she still missed home and being with other people. Now, as she marched towards the stink of the factories looming in the skies, she wished they didn't remind her of what she'd left behind.

They arrived at a long path leading to the factory gates. Jack pointed ahead of them.

'Do we go around or through it?'

Ella glanced at the clouds of pollution hanging over them. Small bits of it drifted down and into her lungs, and she let out a prolonged violent cough.

'I'd rather avoid it, but I suppose it will be quicker. And

someone inside might know where Pandora went or where Merlin is.'

Jack scrunched his nose at her.

'What do you think happened to those babies?'

She thought about it for a second.

'Perhaps the storks took them to their mothers.'

While he considered that, Ella checked her phone, surprised to see the time had moved on by twenty minutes. She showed it to him.

'I'm getting old again.'

He pointed at the building.

'Maybe it's because you're close to things from your world.'

She hadn't considered that. Perhaps inside the factory, she'd find a door to take her home. When Ella had followed Pandora to this place, she'd given no thought to getting back, assuming she'd only have to think about it for it to happen.

'Let's see what's inside.'

Jack grimaced, but strode next to her as they took the path to the entrance. As they went, she noticed tiny shapes dotted along the side, miniature versions of clothing: shoes, socks, shirts, trousers, skirts, coats, gloves and jackets.

Jack saw them as well.

'Perhaps small people work in the factory.'

They continued walking until they reached the open gate. The sound of machines burst from the building, a loud crunching which made Ella shiver. She ignored her doubts and marched straight inside with Jack following her.

Lights hanging from the walls and the roof illuminated the building. On either side were giant machines clicking and turning, but she couldn't work out what they were doing. She was about to move closer when a strange sight scampered forward.

'Are you here for the tour?'

Ella's mouth hung open, her tongue tied in knots against her lips. A colossal head wobbled towards her on tiny legs, with even smaller arms waving at her. There was no neck to it, or body; only that head gazing at her. She didn't know what to say, but Jack did.

'Yes, we are. Can you show us around?'

The head bounced up and down, and Ella held her breath in case it broke those legs.

'Of course. I'm Zack, the Forehead here. I'll tell you how it works and answer all your questions.' He smiled at Ella through great white teeth. 'Is this because Empress Pandora wants to build her own factory?'

Ella nodded. 'Yes, we're here on orders from Empress Pandora.'

She glanced at Jack.

'Good, good,' Zack said. 'Let's get this tour started.'

He spun around on his little legs, and they followed him into the building, striding between the crunching machines on either side of them. Ella still couldn't tell what they were doing or see what was producing that foul smell as they went deep into the factory.

Jack whispered in her ear.

'What does Pandora want with this place?'

Before she could reply, Zack stopped them by raising a tiny hand.

'This is where the magic starts. Everything the Empress wants begins here.'

Ella was wondering what that magic was when a conveyer belt trundled and squeaked by her side and brought a shocking sight to them.

A baby!

'What's happening here?' Jack said.

'Watch,' Zack said.

Ella was about to snatch the infant off the conveyor when a large box dropped from the ceiling and covered the child. She grabbed at her chest and shuddered as the box trembled and let out a terrible noise like two cars crashing into each other. A shiver ran down her back as she glared at Zack.

'You're turning them into food?'

Her stomach churned as she fought the urge to throw up. The strange head on legs narrowed his eyes at her and laughed.

'Of course not. These are for the Empress's army.'

7 HEY! (RISE OF THE ROBOTS)

Ella stared at the box as it lifted away and revealed a fully grown naked man sitting there. She blushed a little before turning to Zack.

'Your machines turn babies into adults?'

He seemed confused. 'Isn't that what Empress Pandora wants?'

Jack stepped in. 'Yes, of course, that's why we're here, checking the process is working, you know.'

Relief seeped from Zack's enormous head and he laughed.

'Right, you were only testing me.' He stared at her. 'Don't worry; everything is going to schedule.'

Ella calmed her nerves. 'The army will be ready on time?'

'Yes, yes. Look.' He led them further down the aisle, where they witnessed the process happening again, dozens of times. She gazed each time with her eyes wide enough to fall from her head. The boxes came down, covered the babies, wobbled and gurgled for about thirty seconds before lifting off and revealing the new adults beneath. She'd seen some impossible things become real in the last few days, but this was the most fantastic.

'How does this work?' Ella said.

Zack shook his colossal head so hard, she thought it might pop off his little legs.

'I'm just the Forehead in charge of the production line. The mechanics of it are above my pay grade.'

Jack pointed at one of the shivering adults as the conveyor belt wheeled them away.

'These were all boys. What happened to the girls?'

Zack chuckled. 'Boys are the soldiers. We don't want girls for that.'

Ella forgot about the terrible things she'd witnessed and clenched her fists.

'Girls can fight as well as boys.'

'Just as good, if not better,' Zack said. 'But the Empress wants the girls as intelligence officers because,' he tapped his little hand against the side of his head, 'they have more brains.'

'Where do you get the babies from?' Jack said.

'I don't know, Mr Rabbit. That's the supply chain's responsibility.'

They'd come to the end of the factory and the smell was more pungent. Ella put her fingers over her nose.

'What's that stink?'

'Offcuts,' Zack said. 'For when things go wrong with the process.'

Ella staggered out of the exit, bent over and clutched on to her guts as the sun beat down on her face. The air smelt of electricity as if a thunderstorm was coming. She lifted her head when she heard shouting ahead of her.

Jack stood at her side. 'What's going on over there?'

Zack stepped in front of them.

'That's the robot guards monitoring the electric fence against the protestors.'

Ella moved forward, staring at the twelve-foot tall machines marching next to the fence, which shimmered and sparkled blue. On the other side of it was a group of people, humans, shouting at the robots.

'Why are they protesting?'

Zack waved little fingers at them.

'I don't know. I keep well away from that. You can ask them.'

He turned to go back inside.

'Why don't they just come in through the front gate?' Jack said.

Zack looked at him. 'Every time they try, the guards fry them alive. It's quite a sight, I can tell you.'

Ella stopped herself from punching him.

'How did we get in, then?'

'Well, you're the emissaries from Empress Pandora.' He peered at her. 'Aren't you?'

Jack went to slap him on the shoulder, but didn't.

'Of course we are, my good man. Who else would we be?'

Ella didn't wait for an answer, marching towards the protestors without thinking about what the guards might do. As she got closer, one robot towering above her swivelled its metallic hips and lowered its head. Its eyes pulsed a vibrant red and she waited for it to speak.

But it didn't. Jack did.

'We can't hang around here. Pandora's real emissaries might turn up.'

A thought struck Ella as the robot continued to stare at her.

'We could wait, and then follow them to her.'

Before he could reply, one protestor shouted at them.

'Hey, you, let us in.'

Ella stepped from the automaton and approached the woman.

'What do you want?'

Her face was covered in lines and she had heavy bags under her eyes.

'We want our babies back.' Tears flowed down her cheeks. 'Please let us in to see them. Please.'

The pain in Ella's stomach increased a thousandfold with tiny needles stabbing at every part of her. She turned and marched to the factory, the smell of burning electricity lingering in the air. Her hands hung as fists down at her sides.

Jack rushed to her side. 'Do nothing rash, Ella.'

She stopped and glared at him.

'I won't leave them like this. We have to do something.'

He shook his head. 'We can't help them. Those robot guards will kill us.'

'I don't care about them.'

She stomped inside the factory and found Zack staring at the production line. Thankfully, it was empty of babies.

'What are you?'

'Eh?' Confusion gripped his large eyes. 'What do you mean?'

'You were like me once, weren't you?'

He laughed at her. 'You're a girl. I'm nothing like you.'

'You were human.' She glared at him. 'What happened to you?'

Zack lifted his tiny hands. 'You're babbling, child.'

Ella removed her phone and took a photograph of Zack. Then she showed it to him.

'Where are the rest of your body parts, your shoulders

and chest and stomach? What happens when you eat or drink? Why is your head so big, but your arms and legs are so small?'

He stared at the photo, his eyes glazing over as he lifted tiny fingers to his cheek.

'I..., I don't know.' His hands trembled as he examined his face. 'What's happened to me?'

Ella put the phone back in her pocket, noticing that the time had moved on an hour.

'You were human once, like those people outside, and me, but working here has changed you. You're something different now, with no feelings or concerns for others. Your body is withering away, apart from your head, which your owners need so you can keep running this place. Eventually, you'll die, and they'll replace you with someone else.'

Zack's little legs gave way and he slumped to the ground.

'You're right. I was human once. I lived beyond the fence and was invited inside to find my son.' He gazed at his fingers. 'And they did this to me.'

'Was it Pandora?'

He dropped his head into his tiny hands and sobbed.

'Yes. I remember. The Empress promised me I'd be able to see my child.' He lifted his eyes towards her. 'That was a long time ago. Alfie, my son, is gone, isn't he?'

Ella knelt close to him.

'You can save the ones who are here now, Zack. You can be human again.'

He peered straight into her heart.

'How?'

'Do you know where the generators are for the factory?' He nodded. 'Then all you have to do is turn them off. Do you understand?'

They stood together.

'Yes.'

'What about the electric fence and the robots?' Jack said.

'They're on a separate switch,' Zack replied.

Ella smiled. 'That's easy, then.'

Zack's lips trembled. 'No. A robot guards that.'

Jack slapped his forehead. 'Great.'

Ella took Zack's hand. 'Where are these switches?'

His tiny fingers gripped hers. 'On the next level, upstairs.'

She let go of him. 'Show us the way.'

They followed him as Jack spoke to her.

'What's the plan?'

Ella shrugged. 'We'll make it up as we go along.'

He let out a long sigh as they went up the steps behind Zack.

'Are you the only worker in the factory?' Jack said.

'The only living one. Everything else is automated.' They strode down a corridor until he stopped outside a large door. 'The controls for the generators are inside here.'

She peered at the glass, frosted so she couldn't see through it.

'Is the robot guard as big as the others at the fence?'

'Yes. Twelve foot tall. But there's only one.'

Jack sighed again. 'One's enough.' He turned to Ella. 'Have you made something up yet?'

She rubbed at her chin. 'Perhaps we can distract it while Zack switches everything off.'

Jack shook his head. 'Distract it how?'

Ella spoke to Zack. 'Do the robots speak or think for themselves?'

'I've never heard them talk. All I know is they've been programmed for defence.'

'Defending what?'

'The factory.'

She considered that as she opened the door and they entered the room. It was a large space filled with panels covered in flashing lights and switches. At the far end stood the robot with its back to them.

Zack pointed at it. 'The panel to turn off all the power is the other side of the robot.'

Ella approached it and coughed loudly. It didn't move, so she spoke to it.

'Excuse me. Do you have a name?'

Its neck creaked as it twisted towards her and she wondered how long it had sat like that. It looked the same as the others, but nothing flashed in its eyes, which were darker than a black hole. Then its head moved and the sound came from inside it.

'Machines don't have names, child.'

She wagged her finger at it.

'That's not true. Where I'm from, some do.'

It spoke again, its voice warmer than she'd expected.

'Where do you come from?'

'I'm from Earth. Do you know it?'

'The planet of the humans?'

'Yes, that's right. Did humans build you?'

The robot was silent for twenty seconds.

'That knowledge is not in my memory.'

'What is in your memory?'

'I have only one primary goal: to protect at all costs.'

'To protect what?'

'To protect the factory and what it produces.'

'And what does it produce?'

It shifted its large body towards her. There was no light behind its eyes.

'Humans.'

'Like me?'

'Like you.'

'So what would happen if I tried to shut the factory down?'

'I'd kill you.'

'You'd kill me?'

'Yes.'

'But I'm human. You'd kill a human to protect humans?'

Its head bent forward and she smelt the oil coming from it.

'Yes. No. Yes.' Its body shivered. 'Yes. Yes.'

There was no warmth to its voice now, only a trembling that reminded her of the sound a train makes as it speeds along the tracks.

Then it stopped.

'I think you broke it,' Zack said.

Ella moved closer to it.

'I hope so.'

Then she stepped beyond the frozen machine and saw the power switches for the generators. There were six of them and she reached out for the first one. As she did so, the robot twisted its body towards her. Now she witnessed the fire blazing in its eyes.

'Yes, yes, yes,' it said as it raised a large metallic fist at her.

8 THE CASTLE

Ella held her breath, but didn't wait. She moved from the robot and turned all the switches off while expecting those great fingers to crush her.

But they didn't. The robot stood there, frozen, its fist hovering above her head.

Jack yelped. 'Blimey, crikey, Ella, you gave me a scare.'

Ella finally relaxed her lungs. 'That makes two of us.'

She reached into her pocket and removed the phone. Then she took a selfie of her and the robot, wishing she'd taken more photos on her journey for when she returned home.

Billy will never believe me otherwise.

Zack sat at the feet of the machine.

'Tell the protestors they can come inside now.'

She put her hand on his cheek.

'They're not protestors, Zack. They're parents. Just like you.'

He reached up and squeezed her fingers.

'Thank you.'

They left him and exited the building. Outside, the

people must have realised something had changed as they were already tearing the fence down when Ella and Jack got there. A few appeared fearful of the frozen robots, but the rest ran past and headed for the factory.

Jack stood at Ella's side. 'What now?'

She looked into the sky and shielded her eyes from the sun.

'We find Merlin.'

'You need to head north along the Round Table Road for the castle.' She turned to see Zack behind her. 'Rumours say that's where Merlin is.' He glanced towards the people running into the building. 'I'll do what I can to help them and make sure this factory is destroyed.'

They thanked him and left through the gap the crowd had created in the fence. Ella and Jack walked away, flanked by two rows of dead robots. Outside the perimeter, they headed down the hill towards the village in the distance.

'That must be where they got the babies from,' Jack said.

She nodded. 'It seems likely.'

It took twenty minutes to reach the houses and the emptiness of the place. She'd loved studying history at school and, from watching videos, recognised the buildings as being from a different time to hers, which was strange as the crowd was wearing modern clothes.

It was eerie moving through the centre, where nothing stirred but them. It was nearly as chilling as what she'd seen inside the factory.

Nearly, but not quite.

She was glad when they left the place and found the road they needed for their journey. Jack pointed at the sign above them.

'The Round Table Road. I guess this is for us.'

'Yes,' Ella said. 'Shall we eat on the way?'

He reached into the bag and handed her a pack of sandwiches and a bottle of water. He stuck to a carrot.

'Can we at least make a plan this time?'

'A plan for Merlin? We won't need to. Merlin is one of the good guys from British history.'

He nibbled on his food and looked unconvinced.

'Tell me about him.'

Ella ate as she walked, chewing on a piece of strong cheddar cheese.

'In the legends about King Arthur in Great Britain, Arthur was the head of the kingdom Camelot and the Knights of the Round Table. He had the help and advice of a powerful wizard named Merlin.'

'So, he's not real?'

She stopped to laugh without choking on her food, gazing at Jack as her sides shook.

'Says the talking rabbit.'

He laughed as well.

'I think talking rabbits are real everywhere but your world, Ella Finn.'

She took a swig of the water.

'When we first met, you said you didn't know what a rabbit was.'

His whiskers twitched as he spoke.

'Are you sure? I don't remember that.'

Was she sure?

'I believe so, but my memory has been fuzzy since I came here. I think it's playing tricks on my mind.'

'It's not just you, Ella. Everywhere is going through some strange changes.'

'What do you mean?'

'Well, all these places we've been to wouldn't normally be like this. We'd have to go through a gateway to get to them, whereas now they're all joined together.'

She thought about that. They'd travelled through four different lands: those of the snarks, the penguins, the cats, and the factory. She thought of it like playing a game of Monopoly and going from one square to another.

'I hope we don't go straight to jail,' she said out loud.

'What?' Jack said.

'Nothing. Just something I remembered from home.' She had some more water. 'What do you think is happening?'

'It's only a guess, but it seems to me all the places we've visited might have been dragged into Everywhere from their original locations, and the inhabitants are unaware of it.'

She thought about it as they went.

'Did this only start recently?'

He nodded. 'Yes. Just before I met you.'

That's what she'd guessed.

'It must have something to do with Pandora coming here. She told me she could travel from her world to mine directly. Perhaps she lied, but I don't think so. She might have arrived here by accident, or she made a mistake, and I think it must have weakened her even further.'

'What about that factory? Zack knew of her and seemed to have met her before. How long has she been planning this army, and where was that place from?'

These were questions Ella didn't yet have answers for, but she was determined to find them.

'We can ask Merlin when we meet him.'

'So, you have a plan?'

'Yes. We'll ask him what he knows about Pandora and how to stop her.'

It had sounded like a good idea in her head, but Jack's expression as they continued along the road told her he wasn't too impressed with it.

'Tell me about this Round Table and how it connects to Merlin.'

Ella dug deep into what she remembered of her mother's books about British myths and legends.

'King Arthur's court was Camelot, and the Round Table was where he and his Knights ruled the land, I think.' Some details were fuzzy in her brain, and she got them mixed up with a comedy film her parents used to watch. 'It was a long time ago, but most people, historians and such, don't believe it was real.'

'What about you?'

She stared at the talking rabbit.

'I'm not sure what's real and what isn't anymore.'

They came to the end of the road and saw a great field ahead of them. In the distance was a castle surrounded by a lake. Jack pointed at it.

'That must be the place.'

She peered at it through the meadows.

'There's a church in front of it.'

'Perhaps there'll be people there we can talk to about Merlin.'

She agreed. 'Let's go there first.'

They marched on, with Ella enjoying the smell of the flowers as they went. They filled her head with memories of home and her parents' extensive garden near their London laboratory. She pictured them both, feeling guilty about how she'd left them behind to go to Everywhere.

The memory of her mother's smile warmed her heart as they reached the cemetery. She glanced at the gravestones as they went, unable to read most of them because the names were faded, but she noticed each one had the image of a sword on it.

'There must have been great friendship between the Knights and the King,' Jack said.

She ran her fingers over the stone of the closest grave.

'I don't think it ended well for any of them.'

'Oh,' Jack said. 'Why not?'

Ella shrugged. 'I'm not sure. It was something my mum told me.'

They continued through the cemetery as the sky darkened. The threat of rain was heavy in the air as they both increased their pace. The temperature turned chilly as they reached the bridge across the lake.

'At least the gate is open,' Jack shouted as they ran towards it.

By the time they got there, the heavens had opened and a torrential downpour was falling everywhere. Ella pulled the collars of her jacket to her face as she sheltered under the castle's stone entrance.

Jack leant against the wall. 'It's empty here. Do you think the place is abandoned?'

She hoped not.

They ran through the courtyard as the rain battered their heads, throwing themselves inside the castle as Jack barged the door open and they stumbled into a corridor. The wind howled behind them, with a great gust blowing her into a suit of armour. She fell on to it with her arms in front of her face, her elbows banging into the metal as she and it went crashing down. The sound echoed through the space as Ella pushed the armour off her and stared at Jack's grin as he dripped water over the ground.

'It's okay, don't worry about me.'

He stuck out his paw as he laughed. She grabbed it and he dragged her up.

'At least we won't have to ring a bell to let people know we're here.'

She swept the dust from her clothes and winced at the bruise growing on her hip. She sneezed as she peered at the walls on either side of them, gazing at the paintings hanging from them. Each one was of a Knight in armour, holding a shield or sword, while staring out of the frame. Some had dragons or other beasts at their feet, while others gripped on to skulls or bones.

She sneezed again as they continued into the castle, striding down the corridor until they came to a magnificent hall. Hanging above the entrance were great tapestries depicting the Knights in action, defeating dragons and enemies, taking part in jousts, or sitting around the Round Table.

They walked underneath the tapestry showing Arthur being proclaimed King and entered the hall. Ella took a deep breath as she stared at the Round Table in the centre of the room. She looked over and imagined it full of Knights with King Arthur at the head.

She stepped inside, her feet kicking up dust from the floor, which swirled around her face and made her sneeze once more. Jack handed her a handkerchief.

Ella thanked him and took it, wiping the cloth across her lips and nose. There was dizziness banging at the back of her skull, which made her legs wobble as she strode towards the Round Table.

Her hand touched wood and more dust clung to her fingers. Jack stood by her side and looked around the hall while she felt the ancient surface beneath her skin. It was as if she was connected to centuries of British history and mythology for one second, hearing the names rush through her mind: Arthur, Merlin, Guinevere, Galahad, Lancelot, Mordred, Excalibur, and Camelot.

She moved to the table's head and put her hand on the seat as Jack explored the great hall. She watched him checking every space as she pulled out a chair and sat down. She stared across the Round Table, seeing the ghosts of the past as Jack returned.

'This place is empty, Ella. I don't think anyone's been here for a long time.'

Her heart sank as she realised they'd gone there for nothing, and they were no closer to finding Pandora. Her mind was so full of disappointment, she nearly didn't hear the footsteps coming towards them.

'Are you a queen?'

The voice was old, carrying a thousand years of history in every word. Ella jerked up to see the ancient Knight approach them. Only he was more than a Knight since he wore a crown.

'King Arthur!' she shouted.

'At your service, My Lady.'

She froze in the seat, unsure of how to address him. Should she stand and curtesy or do nothing? She'd seen British Royalty on the TV many times, and ordinary people like her were constantly bowing or curtseying to them.

Jack solved her problem by stepping forward and offering his hand to him.

'It's a great pleasure to meet you, Your Majesty.'

Arthur bellowed out a hearty laugh.

'A talking rabbit as tall as a man, now I've seen everything.'

Ella snapped out of her daze and jumped from the seat.

'King Arthur, we need your help.'

He finished shaking Jack's paw and stared at her.

'Are you English, my child?'

'Yes, Your Majesty. My name is Ella Finn. Great Britain is in grave danger and only you can save it.'

'Well, that sounds serious.' He glanced across the Round Table. 'The three of us should sit down and talk about this danger you speak of.'

They did that and, because she didn't want to appear rude, she asked where everyone was. He clasped his hands.

'I'm the only one left, child. All the others are long dead.'

'Oh.' She didn't know how else to react. 'Do you know where Merlin is, Your Majesty?'

'Merlin?' He peered at her. 'What do you want with the Great Mage?'

She told him about Pandora and how they needed Merlin's knowledge to defeat her. Arthur's eyes darkened as he replied.

'If that's the case, then I'm afraid you've travelled here for nothing, Ella Finn.'

Her heart sank. 'Why?'

'Because there is no Merlin. There never has been.'

'What?' Ella and Jack said together.

King Arthur stood and waved his hand in the air. Ella sat there in amazement as a golden glow appeared out of nowhere, forming a circular shape. Her mouth was wide open when the glow split in two. Then, with great speed, one half sped over and wrapped itself around her, while the other did the same to Jack. Ella tried to flex her body and move her legs, but she couldn't.

She was imprisoned inside the golden glow, and so was Jack.

'Why are you doing this?'

Arthur wagged his finger and the shimmering lasso tightened around Ella. Pain shot through her chest and arms as she struggled to breathe. He moved towards her.

'Don't worry; all will become clear soon.' He put his hand on her cheek, and it shimmered and changed shape against her skin. 'And you'll have plenty of time to listen to my story.'

Ella watched his face change before she passed out.

9 ABRACADABRA

Ella woke with her head inside a washing machine set to maximum heat. She blinked and realised she was lying on silk covers on a giant bed.

'This is much better than the last prison we were in.' She sat up to see Jack tucking into a vast plate of vegetables. 'Are you hungry, Ella?'

She slipped off the bed and rubbed at her stomach.

'Actually, I am.'

Ella joined him at the table and he shared the food with her.

'I woke up twenty minutes ago and found this here.' He pointed at a jug near her. 'And there's beer.'

She took water instead. 'I'm too young for that, Jack.'

'Of course,' he said. 'I sometimes forget how old you are.' He glanced at the door in the corner. 'How are we going to get out of here?'

She chewed on the best lettuce she'd ever tasted.

'I don't know yet. We have to work out what Arthur wants.'

'There is no Arthur.' A woman appeared out of

nowhere next to the table. Jack jerked forward and spat bits of potato all over himself. 'Just like there's no Merlin, and there never has been.'

Ella stared at her, looking over the woman's brown eyes and expression, which said she wasn't to be messed with. She figured it was best to keep her talking until she could work out an escape.

'What do you mean there's never been a Merlin? Was he a myth all along?'

'In a way, yes.' The woman lifted her hand and an apple floated from the table and into her fingers. 'People could never handle the truth, so they rewrote it to suit their version of history.'

Ella felt something invisible pressing on her ribs and, even though she couldn't see it, she knew the golden lasso was still around her.

'What does that mean?'

She used to like riddles, but now she was getting sick of them.

The woman bit into the apple, crunching on a piece before answering.

'My name is Mary Lynne. Does that answer your question?'

Ella thought about it for two seconds.

'Mary Lynne is Merlin?'

The woman nodded. 'I know; it's that simple.'

'Hang on,' Jack said. 'Why would all the books say it was a man called Merlin when it was you all the time?'

She put the apple on the table.

'Because men wrote all the books, my dear talking rabbit.'

Ella sat back in the chair and tried to stop the thumping in her head.

'Do you have any painkillers?'

Mary Lynne looked at her.

'Do you have a headache?' Ella nodded. 'I'm sorry about that. It sometimes happens when people encounter magic for the first time.' She waved a finger at her and the pain disappeared. 'Is that better?'

'Yes, but that doesn't mean I forgive you for imprisoning us.' She glanced at the food on the table. 'No matter how nice it is in here.'

'I'm sorry again. But I had no choice.'

'Why?' Jack said.

Mary Lynne sighed. 'People don't realise what a curse it is to be immortal.' She reached for the apple, but pulled away. 'Living forever is a terrible thing when you have to witness everyone you love dying in front of you.' She glanced at the ceiling. 'It becomes so lonely, having nobody to share your life with. The isolation drives one a little crazy.'

Ella stared at their captor.

'So you've imprisoned us so you won't feel lonely?'

Mary Lynne leant towards her.

'It's terrible, I know, but you must understand why I did it. I can't live another day on my own.'

'Why don't you leave here and go where others are?' Ella said.

'That's impossible. If I spend too much time away from Camelot, I lose my magic.' She ran her hand over the table. 'I'm tied to these walls forever. And even if I left, people would still die around me.'

Ella peered at her. 'But we'll die, eventually.'

'Yes, I understand that. But you're only a young girl, and I can make you live an extra two or three hundred years.' She looked at Jack. 'And probably longer for the talking rabbit.'

Heat surged through Ella's cheeks.

'It's not right and you know it.'

Mary Lynne got out of her seat.

'I'm sorry, but it is what it is. I'm sure we'll become good friends in time.'

Before Ella could argue, the woman who wasn't Merlin disappeared.

'Great,' Jack said.

'Why are people always lying to me?'

Ella grabbed a bun, ripped it in half and spread a significant chunk of butter over it, then got up to check out the room. Apart from the table and two beds, there was a large bookcase against the far wall. She bit into the bread and ran her fingers over the spines of the books.

'Is there at least something decent to read on there?' Jack said.

Ella pulled a few of them out and skimmed through the pages.

'It depends on what you like. These are all about King Arthur and Merlin.'

'Don't you mean Mary Lynne?'

Ella took a few of them to the table.

'Do you think she was telling the truth?'

'I don't see why not.' He rubbed at his chest. 'There's no need for her to lie now she's got us locked up.' He chewed on a piece of pineapple. 'Even if it's in apparent luxury.' He reached for a book. 'Perhaps there's something in one of these which will tell us how to beat her.'

Ella continued eating the bread.

'I have a better idea.' He put down the hardcover and

looked at her. 'After all this time we've spent together, I know nothing about you, Jack.'

His whiskers moved as he smiled at her.

'What would you like to know, Ms Ella Finn?'

'Well, for starters, tell me where you're from. What's your world like? Are there only rabbits there?'

'Oh no.' He picked a piece of stray carrot from his teeth and dropped it on to the floor. 'There are many animals there, and everyone gets along famously.'

She narrowed her eyes at him.

'Is that true?'

He laughed. 'No. We have our fair share of troubles, just like anywhere else. That's why I do my job.'

Considering where she was and the fact there was an invisible chain around her chest, she still relaxed.

'What's your job?'

He stuck out his chest. 'I'm a police rabbit, a detective.'

'Wow. That's impressive, Jack. Is there a lot of crime there?'

'Oh yes. Carrot theft is rampant. And not just with rabbits. Dogs are the worst. They eat anything.'

'And all the animals can talk in your world?'

'Of course.'

Ella grinned. 'I'd like to visit it.'

'You will. And I'll introduce you to my wife and children.'

'You have a family?'

He shook his head. 'Silly me. I should have shown you the photos.' He removed his mobile, flicked through the screen, and then handed it to her. 'I'm assuming you know how to use a phone?'

Ella nodded. 'Yes, if it's the same as mine.'

It looked like the same make as hers as she stared at the

screen. The first picture was of Jack outside, in a park some-where, standing next to a rabbit in a pretty floral dress.

'That's my wife, Ruth. And the other photos are the kids, Lily and Olive. They're twins, eight years old. Ruth is a doctor.'

She studied the pictures, a warm feeling flowing through her as she stared at the examples of happy family life. It brought her joy even though there was still a hollow echo clawing at her chest.

She handed him the phone. 'Do you miss them?'

'Every day.'

'So why don't you go back to them?'

'Because I'm helping you on a case. I can't leave you on your own.'

Ella put her hand on his paw. 'How did you end up in Everywhere, Jack?'

His grin warmed her heart. 'Now that's a funny story. I was chasing a group of carrot thieves across a field, dogs who split into two groups. I was deciding which to follow when I saw a strange sight in the grass.'

'What was it?'

'Now, Ella, you must understand that, in my world, we only know of humans through storybooks and myths.'

'Humans are fairy tales?'

'Yes. At least, they were until I saw a small one in that grass.'

'A small human?'

'A girl, about twelve inches tall. She gazed at me before running away.'

'What did you do?'

'I had to choose between the criminals and a tiny human from legend. It was no choice, really.'

'You followed her?'

'Of course, until she disappeared down a hole in the ground. I didn't hesitate and jumped after her and ended up in Everywhere.'

'Was it your first time here?'

'Yes.' Confusion rippled through his eyes. 'Yet, somehow, I understood everything about the place as soon as I arrived.'

'What happened to the tiny human you followed?'

'I don't know. I never saw her again.'

'Okay. Well, you're a detective, and I can be clever if I try hard enough. Let's see if we can come up with a plan to get out of here.' She grabbed a book. 'I think you're right, and there might be something in one of these to help us.'

Before she started, Ella checked her phone and noticed time was frozen again. According to it, she'd spent an hour in Everywhere, but she knew it was at least two days.

They sat for hours, going through a dozen books between them, but finding nothing of use, apart from mentions of potential enemies of Arthur and Merlin. She opened one book, laid it on to the table and pointed at an illustration.

'Here, Morgan le Fay stands in front of a loom on which she's woven an enchanted robe, designed to consume the body of King Arthur by fire. In some accounts, she's Arthur's greatest enemy and the mother of his son, Mordred, who kills Arthur in battle. She's also described as possessing great magic.'

Jack examined the page. 'If Merlin was a woman, our captor Mary Lynne, can we believe anything in these books?'

'Probably not, but there's sometimes a little truth in fairy tales and legends.'

'Indeed. Like me following a tiny human down a hole.'

Ella got up from the table and went to the window, staring out across the moat and over the meadows.

'I might have an idea.'

He closed the book with a thump of the pages.

'I knew you would.'

She turned to him. 'But we have to get out of here and outside.'

As she was considering how to do that, there was a knock on the door.

Jack glanced at her. 'Has that been open all this time?'

She laughed. 'Who knows?' She held a hardback close to her chest and stared at the door. 'Come in.'

There was no sound of a lock turning as it opened. Ella had prepared herself for anything but the striking red-headed woman who entered. She wore a beautiful blue medieval dress, stitched with shimmering gold lace.

'My name is Guinevere. Will you accompany me to the Round Table?'

Jack and Ella glanced at each other. Ella kept hold of the book as she moved towards the woman.

'You're Queen Guinevere, wife to King Arthur?' The woman nodded. 'Do you know where Merlin is?'

'Of course.' The gold in her dress continued to shimmer, and Ella had to use her hand to keep the light from dancing into her eyes. 'Mary Lynne is waiting for you at the Round Table. If you follow me, I'll take you to her.'

She turned and walked to the door.

Jack sidled up to Ella. 'How does this fit into your plan?'

'I don't know yet.'

But she was ready to do some lying of her own.

10 FIGHT THE POWER

They followed Guinevere out of the room into the corridor. Ella scanned the area, searching for a way to escape, before remembering the invisible bonds binding her.

I'll stick to my plan.

They walked behind the Queen, not saying a word until they reached the Great Hall.

'I hope you enjoyed your rest and food.'

Mary Lynne stood at the table, wearing a similar dress to Guinevere, except it was bright red with silver shimmers. Ella would have found them beautiful if she hadn't been there as a prisoner. As she marched in, she realised she was still carrying the hardback. She moved to the Round Table and placed the book on it.

'Jack and I have been thinking about your proposal.'

To keep us prisoners for three hundred years.

Mary Lynne smiled at them.

'Good, good. And what have you decided?'

'We'll stay with you.' *As if we have any choice.* 'But only with a few conditions.'

Their captor sat at the top of the table.

'Go on.'

Ella sat opposite, with Jack next to her.

'We can't be cooped up in this castle all the time. It's no good for a young girl, and definitely not for a rabbit.'

'Okay,' Mary Lynne said. 'What do you suggest?'

Ella placed one hand on the book.

'I've been reading about the chivalrous tournaments you used to have at Camelot. Jack and I think you should start them again for our entertainment.'

She looked at Jack, who seemed confused.

Mary Lynne smiled at her. 'I see. And how would we do that with only us here?'

Ella returned her grin. 'Guinevere.'

'What about her?'

'She's not real, is she?' Ella glanced at Guinevere for a response, but there was nothing. 'You've used your magic to conjure her up for us.'

'Not just for your benefit. She and the others keep me company in my isolation.'

'If you have them, why do you need us?' Jack said.

Mary Lynne stood and went to Guinevere.

'Whatever I summon, whoever I make real, is from my memories. They can't say anything new to me or help me with my loneliness beyond being an echo of what I've already lost.'

It was what Ella had guessed.

'But you can do something similar outside for a jousting tournament?'

'Of course. Would you like me to show you?'

Ella agreed. 'We might as well.'

Jack was about to speak when Mary Lynne snapped her fingers and they disappeared. They reappeared in the middle of the meadow, surrounded by Knights on horses and a baying public shouting from the stands. Ella and Jack sat in the front row with Guinevere, while Mary Lynne was behind them, wearing a crown, on her throne.

Jack leant into Ella. 'Is this part of your plan?'

She whispered to him, 'Do you remember her telling us her magic is tied to the castle?' He nodded. 'Well, if that's so, the further we are away from it, the weaker she'll be. Do you understand?'

He glanced at the castle behind them.

'How much further do you think we need?'

She pointed to the edge of the meadow and beyond the run for the jousting tournament.

'That should do us.'

'How do we get there?'

She smiled at the fake Guinevere.

'I'm working on it.'

The sound of horns blew through the air as an announcement came for the first joust of the day.

'Sir Cador versus Sir Dagonet.'

Ella watched as two heavily armoured Knights entered the field, carrying lances and riding horses. She was feeling sorry for the poor animals, having to carry so much weight until she remembered they weren't real.

The fake crowd cheered as the combatants retreated to opposite ends of the meadow about three hundred yards apart. Ella peered into the cheering masses, seeing the ones closest to her were fully formed, but the further out she looked, the more people shimmered in and out of existence like wisps of smoke floating through the air.

It must mean Mary Lynne's magic is not strong enough to hold all the ghost people's forms for too long.

Then Ella glanced down at where she sat and wondered if her seat and the rest of the stand would collapse if the magician were distracted. Now was not the time to find out. Ella focused on the joust as the Knights charged at each other. They might not have been real, but she still felt and heard the horses charging across the grass, and the ground shook when the lances smashed into their shields. The crowd cheered as the Knights came away unscathed and turned around for a second attempt.

Jack whispered to her, 'Perhaps we should ask if we can have a go as a way of getting down there.'

She thought about that during the next six jousts. As she was considering how dangerous it might be, Mary Lynne appeared between her and Jack.

'Is this entertaining enough for you?'

Ella moved a little so she wasn't pressed up against the magician.

'We want to have a go.'

The whole of the fake crowd stopped moving as their creator let out a huge bellowing laugh.

'You two? You wouldn't make it up on to the horses.'

Ella glared at her. 'I've ridden a horse before.'

Her mother had taken her riding once. Admittedly, it was only a pony, and she was on it for a minute before falling off, but nobody needed to know that.

Mary Lynne gazed at her with new admiration.

'Really? And you want to joust each other?'

'It was my idea,' Jack said. 'We're getting bored otherwise.' He inched closer to the magician. 'Perhaps you could conjure up a couple of steeds appropriate for our size.'

'And have you ridden before, Mr Rabbit?'

'Oh yes, all the time. I'm quite the jockey back home.'

Mary Lynne looked between the two of them before deciding.

'Very well.'

Then she snapped her fingers and all three of them disappeared.

Ella was on a small pony when she reappeared, but there was no armour, and in her hands were a plastic lance and spear. Jack was the same sitting opposite her.

'I don't want either of you harming yourselves,' Mary Lynne said next to them. 'But I must admit, I'm intrigued by this challenge.'

Ella stared at her as the ponies moved away from each other.

'Who do you think will win?'

The magician laughed. 'Never bet against a rabbit.'

The steeds separated until they were two hundred yards apart. Mary Lynne clicked her fingers to return to her seat in the stand.

Jack shouted at Ella. 'Shall we run now?'

'Let's practise first to get used to these ponies.'

It seemed like a good idea, even though she was itching to leave the meadow and get as far away as possible. The saddle was uncomfortable under her, so she squirmed on the pony as it trotted in the field. It appeared to want to go anywhere but towards Jack. She pulled on the reins, but it wasn't easy to control the pony while she was holding on to the lance and shield.

She pushed her head into the pony's ear.

'Don't worry. This will be over soon.'

As it steadied underneath her and turned forward, she wondered if she was talking to the little horse or herself. It picked up speed, going from a trot to a sprint in a matter of seconds. Ella gripped on to the plastic weapons in her hands and peered at Jack, heading towards her in a rush.

Am I supposed to hit him?

Behind her was the sound of the fake crowd cheering.

The pony charged forward, the energy in its back vibrating through her legs. The wind pushed up against her head and she smelt the petals of the wildflowers in the meadow.

Ella's head was spinning and excitement surged through her. This might have been a trick to get away from Mary Lynne, but it was the best she'd felt in a long time. Her smile was as wide as the horizon as she charged towards her friend, laughing as she saw Jack's broad grin as he sped for her. Both of them had their lances aimed at the other, and Ella sensed the electricity in the air.

The wind rushed at her as the distance to Jack disappeared and they readied to barge into each other. The adrenalin surging through her was reminiscent of the time she took a rollercoaster ride with her mother, and they fell a hundred feet towards the ground while others screamed around them.

That noise rang through her head as she saw the excitement in Jack's eyes and the tips of their lances only yards apart. She kept on going, pulling hard on the reins as she became possessed by the occasion, forgetting what they were there to do and thrusting her lance at his chest. It was only plastic, yet she realised it would be painful when it hit.

She pulled away at the last moment.

They missed each other by inches, their steeds gasping opposite each other as they came to a halt. Jack was out of breath when he spoke.

'For one second, I thought you were going to hit me.'

Ella sucked great gulps of air into her lungs.

'So did I.' She glanced at the cheering crowd behind them. 'But it must have convinced Mary Lynne.'

He guided his pony close to her.

'Do you think we're far enough away that our invisible magic chains won't work?'

She nodded to the trees at their side.

'Maybe, but getting over there will be better.'

'How do you want to do it?'

'We'll do another charge, just like that one, but at the last moment, we pull the ponies over there. Then we jump off and run for it.'

Jack nodded as the crowd shouted for more. They pulled their steeds around and prepared for the next charge. They were too far away to see Mary Lynne's face, and Ella expected the distance would help them when they fled. Even if Mary Lynne magically appeared next to them, Ella hoped she'd be too far from the castle for her magic to work properly.

She steadied her pony, and then she charged again, ready to ditch the lance and spear before jumping from the steed. She gripped on to the reins as Jack got closer to her. The time seemed to slow down as she prepared to flee from the field.

Ella waited.

And waited.

Then, when she saw the whites of Jack's eyes, she dragged the pony to the side and towards the trees. As he rode next to her, they threw away their weapons. The plastic bounced off the ground as the edge of the meadow approached. They jumped from the ponies at the same time.

Ella landed on her feet and rolled over. Grass stuck to her as she tumbled through it, only stopping as she hit the bottom of a tree. Pain stabbed at her ribs as she grabbed at the bark and bits of it cut into her fingers. Blood dripped from them as she looked up to see Jack sprinting towards her.

'Come on, Ella. We're nearly out of the field.'

She ignored the ache in her side and jumped up. She was running close behind him as a strange thought struck her.

Rabbits are fast.

She was laughing at this as the edge appeared a few feet away.

Then invisible hands grabbed at her chest and pulled her back as if she was attached to a giant rubber band. She flew backwards, past her abandoned pony, until she hit another tree. Ella crumpled to the floor as Jack landed next to her.

'How stupid do you think I am?'

Mary Lynne was looming over her as Ella passed out.

11 HOWL

Ella blinked at the hundreds of candles flickering across the Round Table. Jack was sitting next to her, both of them staring at Mary Lynne chewing on a chicken leg.

'You need to accept your life is here with me now. Silly attempts at escape will only end up hurting you.'

An invisible force pressed against Ella's chest as cold fingers clutched at her heart. She could only think of one thing to say.

'Where do you get all of this food from?'

Mary Lynne dropped the chicken bone on to the table.

'Don't worry; there's plenty here to keep us going for a long time. There are plentiful crops and livestock inside the castle.'

Ella tried to ignore the pain running through her.

'It doesn't matter how long you imprison us. We'll try to escape every day. You can't stop that.'

The magician curled her lips. 'What am I going to do with you?'

'I have a better idea,' Ella said. 'One that will suit us all.'

Mary Lynne shook her head. 'I'm in no mood for more tricks.'

Ella removed her mobile from her jacket and flicked through the photos until she found what she wanted. She slid it across the table to her jailor.

'Have a look at that.'

Mary Lynne picked it up and Ella noticed she wasn't surprised to see a phone. She stared at the screen.

'This is you with a piece of metal with a human face. So?'

'That's a robot. Even if you keep us with you for three hundred years...' she didn't use the word prisoners, 'we'll die eventually, and you'll be back where you started, on your own again. But I know how you can have company for the rest of your life.'

Mary Lynne's nose twitched. 'How is that possible?'

Ella pointed at the photo on her phone.

'There's a place where there are dozens of these robots, mechanical people who, with your magic, will never break down, and you can program them to think and do whatever you want. You can even tell them to think for themselves. There's a man there called Zack who'll teach you how to use the robots. You can help him as well.'

'Help him how?'

'You'll know when you see him.'

The magician moved closer to her.

'Where is this place?'

Ella felt her plan coming together.

'I'll tell you when you promise to let Jack and me go.'

'Why should I trust you?'

'What have you got to lose? You know we can't escape from you.'

Mary Lynne peered at the photo.

'And these robots will live forever?'

'They'll live as long as you.'

The magician picked up the phone and gazed at the screen. For one second, Ella thought her plan had failed until their captor spoke.

'Take me to this place and I'll release you from your bonds.'

'Both of us?'

'Yes.'

'And you won't try to harm us again?'

'I won't.'

Ella smiled. 'Okay. Can you conjure up something for us to get there?'

'What would you like?'

Jack put up his hand.

'I have an idea.'

––––––––––––

THE AIR BLEW Ella's hair away from her face as they soared above the clouds. She peered down as they flew over the village and headed for the factory. Jack, sitting behind, shouted into her ear.

'How do you like flying on a winged horse?'

She glanced over at the beating wings, which lowered them outside the building.

'I can get used to it. I'm just glad the magic got us this far, and it didn't disappear below us halfway here.'

'Don't worry about that, Ella.' Mary Lynne stepped off her magical steed and approached them. 'And it will take you back beyond Camelot for the next stage of your journey.'

'Our journey?'

The magician smiled at them.

'In your search for Pandora.'

'You know about that?'

Mary Lynne held up her hands.

'It's known across every land. Some say you are trying to recruit an army.' She glanced at Jack. 'Staying with me would be better for you.'

Ella narrowed her eyes at her.

'You made a promise.'

'One which I intend to keep. I just thought you might have wanted to stay and help me with the robots instead of rushing into Pandora's murderous embrace.'

'What do you know about her?'

'Pandora? She's before my time, but I've heard the myths and legends. She believes herself to be the Creator of all things.'

'And you don't?'

Mary Lynne shook her head.

'Many beings set themselves up as gods, but I've lived for an eternity, and I'm yet to meet the one True God.'

'Do you know where Pandora is?'

'Keep heading north and you'll find her. Pandora is at the end of Everywhere, at the spot where there is nowhere else to go.'

'How can I defeat her?'

The magician's nose twitched again.

'Her blood flows through you, child. That's where you'll discover your answer.'

'Great,' Jack said.

They left Mary Lynne talking to Zack as they pulled on their flying horses' reins and headed towards Camelot. Within half an hour, they'd left the factory and the castle behind them. No sooner had they climbed down than the winged creatures vanished.

There was no path or road to help them on their way this time, just a meadow to stroll through before they reached a wooded area.

'This reminds me of home,' Jack said as they walked between the trees.

Ella took in the smells of the countryside: the fresh grass, the flowers, and the mushrooms dotted around their feet. Branches rustled above them as she glanced up to see squirrels jumping from tree to tree.

'What will you do when this is over?' she said to him.

He scrutinised the ground ahead as he replied.

'Return to my family. And you?'

She ran her fingers across the bark of a tree, enjoying its touch against her skin. After being inside the factory, and then imprisoned at the castle, she was glad to be outside again.

'The same. I'll go back to my parents and tell them about my adventures here.'

She watched a bird staring at her from the trees and wondered if they'd get home at all.

'Grabbit, grabbit, I smell a rabbit.'

Ella spun around to see where the voice was coming from, but there was nobody there.

'Did you hear that, Jack?'

He reached down next to her and grabbed a large branch.

'I'm still shivering from it.'

They stood back to back and scanned everywhere near them. Apart from the rumbling in her belly, the place was silent.

'Let's get out of these trees,' she said.

But neither of them moved. And the voice came again.

'Fee, fi, fo, furl, I smell the blood of an English girl.'

Ella's spine trembled next to her friend.

'Can you see where it's coming from?'

Jack gripped on to the branch.

'I think it's above our heads.'

They craned their necks up, staring into an empty sky. Ella was ready to move when a marshmallow shaped cloud lowered itself towards them. She inched further into Jack and narrowed her eyes because the sun was so bright.

'Can you see this, Jack?'

'Yes. That cloud is turning into a head.'

The nose appeared first, then the cheeks, followed by the mouth, before large pink eyes gazed at them. The rest of the face formed around the other features, revealing a colossal head covered with fur. And then the pink eyes transformed into a fiery red.

It was a wolf.

Jack stumbled back from Ella. He clutched on to the branch and tumbled to the ground. She continued to gaze at the floating wolf's head.

'What do you want?'

'Why, child, I'm only here for one reason.'

'What?'

'To distract you.'

Something rammed into her before she could move. It forced her back and she fell over Jack, smacking into hard mud. He rolled over and took her arm. He'd lost the branch as he grabbed Ella and pulled her up with him.

It wasn't a pretty sight that greeted her.

'Wolves,' she said.

They surrounded them, half a dozen at least, standing eight feet tall on two legs. Their claws were large enough to reach the ground, their teeth all yellow and pointy as spit dripped over their lips. The wolf face that had floated above them had moved, standing three feet away and talking again.

'It's been a long time since we had rabbit stew, hasn't it, lads?' They all howled together. 'And there's a little English girl to chew on as well.' He rubbed at his hairy stomach. 'I hope she isn't as stringy as the last one.'

They wailed again, but Ella wasn't afraid.

'We're under the protection of Merlin, the magician who will strike you down if you touch us.'

Their howls turned into high-pitched laughter, which sent a shiver down her spine. She assumed Floating Head was the leader of the pack as he spoke.

'You mean that old woman stuck in her castle? She won't help you, child.' He reached one long taloned hand towards her. 'She's as scared as you, and just as useless.'

The wolves laughed and made the leaves tremble in the trees. Ella used the moment to reach down for the branch Jack had dropped. She snatched it up and lunged at Floating Head, thrusting the sharp end into the middle of his guts.

He crumbled like a sack of potatoes while the rest of the pack was struck silent.

Then they turned to her and growled as one, a low rumbling noise which shook the mud below her. Until she realised the sound wasn't coming from the wolves, but the earth moving under their feet.

Ella just had time to look down before something came out of the ground and pulled her into it.

12 GOING UNDERGROUND

Ella tumbled through wet earth and tried to grab at the surrounding vines, failing every time as something pulled her further and further underground. Damp dirt grabbed at her throat as she choked and the darkness swallowed her vision. She stopped grabbing at the sides and clutched at her mouth as she struggled to breathe. A thousand heavy metal guitars screamed against her skull, and her brain felt as if it was inside a microwave.

She landed on her backside and a stab of electricity shot through her. Ella rolled into a wall and kept on falling over sharp stones and big clumps of grass. Her legs trembled as she fell over one ledge, and then another, feeling the wind on her face as she rushed for the crevice ahead. Down below it was the roar and the smell of the sea and what she knew would be certain death.

Ella tried to dig her fingers into the mud to stop her from moving towards the edge, but only caught the dirt under her nails. Inside the dark surrounding her was a glint of light from below, and she thought it would be the last thing she'd ever see as she reached the brink.

Bits of her life flashed before her, and she saw her parents as a furry paw grabbed her arm and pulled her back.

'It's a good job I keep myself fit.'

She threw herself into Jack's arms and he helped her up. More light came from below and, as her eyes adjusted to the new surroundings, she looked around her. Underfoot, the loose stones shifted, twisting her ankle and sending shooting pain up her leg. She ignored it and continued to check where they were while still holding on to Jack.

Ella watched her shadow dissolve into the darkness. It was clammy, and the only sounds to greet them were of dripping water and the echo of the sea receding in the distance somewhere.

'What happened?'

'The pigs saved us from the wolves.'

'The pigs?'

'Yes. They dragged us into their world, and now we'll have to find a way out.'

'How do you know this, Jack?'

'Because I've been here before. This is the Pig Underground.'

He stepped down and she followed, recognising they were inside a large cave. Ella placed her hand on the wall for support, walking down the steps by touch alone, fearing she might fall at any second. She was surprised at how smooth the walls and ground were, as if someone had spent hours sanding them clean, but realised the place had probably been untouched for many years, if not forever. She was about to ask Jack where they were going when she saw the lights ahead of them.

As she walked into the Pig Underground, Ella's eyes bulged wide. She followed Jack down the steps, past the candles and lamps illuminating the way. She held her breath as the light grew stronger and she realised what was on the levels surrounding them.

Ominous looming shadows transformed into the heads of pigs staring at her, their long snouts dispensing brief spurts of air in her direction. Every one of them stood there and eyed her with suspicion. Around their feet were many little piglets. Their tiny upturned faces were much happier, more trusting, teeth and eyes shining together at the unexpected guests in their midst.

They continued down the steps until they reached the only flat piece of ground Ella could see, a place overlooking a vast cavern filled with crystal blue light reflected from a pool of water at the side.

'Who's in charge?' Jack asked a pig with bulbous head and eyes which could have been transplanted from an anaemic frog.

'We're all in charge.'

Its voice was dry and raspy, drifting through the Underground and echoing above their heads. Ella couldn't see everything, but it looked like more than a hundred pigs were there. Below where they stood, on the next level down, she saw one who fascinated her, looking like a withered old man. Its skin was grey rather than pink, lines scattered across it resembling moon craters.

'We are a commune run by all,' the pig said as it gazed at her. 'I'm the oldest one here: you can call me Major.'

Splintered illumination from broken lamps ambled up the walls behind him, casting awkward shadows on either side of his wrinkled head. At his side stood an old battery-operated compact disc player, covered in scratches, but with a small green neon light flashing on and off. The timeworn pig noticed where Ella was looking.

'Music is one of the few things we appreciate from the world of humans. There's a comprehensive collection of discs at the bottom of this cavern. You can pick one later if you'd like, but for now, why don't we all sit together and talk about why you're here.'

Jack moved forward. 'You dragged us down here.'

'Yes, we did. Would you rather we left you up there with the wolves?'

As she listened, Ella twisted from side to side to get a better position on the stone, to find a more comfortable spot and remove the bits sticking to her backside.

'What is this place exactly?' she asked Major.

He smiled at her, the lines on his face growing more prominent as his cheekbones extended ever wider.

'You must excuse me for grinning, Miss. I'm not used to having conversations with humans. But to answer your question, we are a community created from all of our kind that have escaped from human farms.'

'This is a pig community?' Ella smiled at the idea of it.

Major grimaced. 'This is a community, yes, but we don't use the other word as our name. That is a human insult, and we prefer to be called Suidae. We share everything we have equally among us, though we are split between two different ideas about approaching the outside world, which is why some will be unhappy with your presence here.'

'Why won't they be happy?' Ella said.

'Some believe we should be more militant in our dealings with humans. Others are content to avoid any contact with humanity. The militant faction are the Mensuidaes, the others are Bolsuidaes: there is constant discussion about how our community will continue in the future.'

'And which group do you belong to?' she said.

He rolled his watery eyes at her and let out a great snort.

'I'm always impartial, my dear lady. It's what comes from being so old.'

Major paused while all around him, the smaller Suidae – Suidaelets - gazed at him with evident admiration. Ella resisted the urge to hug him, distracted by the approaching sound of heavy breathing.

From the shadows, two large shapes emerged and trotted towards them: mean looking hogs with enormous eyes and even larger teeth. A stink of rotten cabbage escaped from the bigger one's mouth as he spoke to them.

'You're not welcome here. The human and the thief must leave.'

Its voice was like the low rumble of thunder.

Ella looked confused. 'Thief?'

'The rabbit,' the big one said. 'He steals across all the lands of Everywhere; everyone knows this.'

She stared at Jack, remembering how he stole the magical jacket from the cats.

But he said he was a police detective in his world.

The bigger hog lunged towards Jack, who flinched as Major stepped between them.

'You know the rules, Gregor. No harm shall come to any of our guests while they're here.'

He lifted his head as he spoke, his authority obvious to all.

'You may be the Elder, but you're not the Leader.'

'Would that be you?' Major asked Gregor.

'There are no leaders here, old man, you know that.'

The smaller hog sidled up to his brother in a show of support.

'We have alliances outside of here. The war is coming,' Gregor said.

'A war against who?' Jack said.

'The glorious revolution will be here soon, and you won't be part of it, thief.' The menace in his tone sliced through the gloom. 'We will avenge centuries of suffering under human hands.'

It was a threat and promise in one. Ella stood and stepped forward, her face shimmering in the candlelight, sorrow and guilt dripping from her voice.

'I wish the rest of my fellow humans would stop eating animals and started treating you with the respect you deserve, but I don't see how any animal uprising could succeed. There are too many of us, and we are far too vicious.'

Gregor snorted again, stomping his hoofs on the ground and pushing his impressive chest out as he spoke.

'It makes no difference now, child. The future has been written, and your kind will have no part in it.'

Ella sensed hundreds of eyes on her as she prepared to discuss peaceful cohabitation with this angry warthog. The idea of it made her smile, but before she could start, Jack stepped forward.

'Thank you for saving us from the wolves, Major, but we won't take up any more of your time.'

'Where will you go next?' Major said.

'To the end of the world,' Ella said.

'Come, I'll escort you outside.' Major lifted his wizened backside from the floor, glanced at the hogs, and moved up the damp steps. Ella gave Jack a knowing look before they followed. They headed up as she felt the hot breath of the hogs wafting on to the nape of her neck.

Her legs ached as they marched upwards for four minutes. She wanted to stop and ask Jack some questions, but stopped herself while they were still underground. It could wait until they got outside.

The sun caressed their eyes as they moved into the light. She watched as all the little pigs scattered out of the way and scampered back inside. Major put his face close to Jack and whispered into his ear. Then the old pig nodded at Ella before disappearing into the earth.

Jack pointed ahead of them.

'I guess we head north again.'

She grabbed his arm before he could move.

'You told me you're a police detective.'

He wriggled out of her grasp.

'I am.'

'You're a police detective and a thief?'

His eyes shrank as he sighed heavily.

'Can't I be both?'

She laughed in his face.

'No, you can't. The police are supposed to be honest and catch criminals. If you're a thief, then you're a criminal. You can't be both.'

He shrugged. 'Life isn't that simple, Ella.' He stared at her while she glowered at him. 'When we find Pandora, how will you prevent her from returning to your world and enslaving it?'

'I don't know.'

'Yes, you do. More than one person has already told you what to do.' He grabbed hold of her hands. 'Pandora's blood is in you, which means her powers are also in you. You'll have to use them to stop her. And you might have to kill her.'

She pulled out of his grasp.

'No. I'll never do that.'

'We'll see, Ella, we'll see.'

He turned from her and started walking north. She watched him go without moving for thirty seconds. And then she followed him.

I won't be a murderer.

I won't.

13   SIZE OF A COW

They followed the beach along the coastline, Ella glancing up at the cliffs as they strode through the edge of the waves in silence. She was waiting for him to speak, but there was nothing until they'd gone more than a mile. Then he stopped and looked at her.

'We'll need to get up top soon.'

'What did you steal from the pigs, Jack?'

His face darkened. 'I'm not a bad person, Ella.'

'I didn't say you were, but you haven't told me the whole truth, have you?'

He turned from her. 'No, but I wanted to.'

'Then tell me now.'

He reached into his pocket and removed the phone.

'Do you remember me telling you about my family?'

She smiled at him. 'Of course. I couldn't forget that, seeing those pictures of your wife and daughters.'

The mobile trembled in his paw as he found the photos and showed her his kids again.

'What I told you about following the tiny human girl into Everywhere is true, only it didn't happen just before I met you, but months ago.' He glanced at the waves lapping their feet. 'I started spending time here, exploring, discovering fantastic new things. And sometimes dangerous new things. My wife became suspicious of where I was. I kept telling her it was extra work for the police, but I'm not sure she believed me. Then, on my last visit before I met you, I was attacked by a masked being who slashed at me with a sword.' He moved his jacket to the side to show the scar across his hip. 'That's when I said I'd never return here.' She took his paw in her hand. 'I needed to be with my family, to watch my children grow up. But then everything changed.'

She gripped on to him.

'What happened, Jack?'

The tears settled into the fur under his eyes.

'Olive got ill. The doctors tried everything, but said there was no hope.' He peered at her. 'So, I came here. There's magic in Everywhere, I know that. I've seen it, so I searched for a cure until I heard about a healing coat. I knew there was a magical jacket in the cat community, so I went there and stole it. Of course, it wasn't what I needed, and I drowned my sorrows in a tavern in the Land of the Goblins. It was in there I overheard a group of rogues talking about the Pig Underground and what they possessed.'

'Which was?'

'A golden fleece with magical healing properties. I wanted to buy it from them, but I had no money. So I did what I had to.'

'You stole it?'

'Yes.'

'What happened to it?'

He sank his head into his hands and sighed deeply before looking at her.

'It was a myth, a legend that wasn't true. All I took was a useless piece of cloth, and in my anger, I threw it into the river.'

'You could have returned it to them.'

'I know, and I'm sorry, Ella, I really am.'

'I believe you, Jack.' She let go of him. 'But you should have told me sooner.'

The sea breeze got up around them, blowing wind through Ella's hair as she took hold of it. It surprised her how she hadn't noticed it had grown so long since she'd been in Everywhere: it was now down to her shoulders. And it was lighter.

Jack smiled at her. 'It will be snow white if you stay here much longer.'

'Is this place changing me?'

He shrugged. 'I don't know, but the atmosphere is different here. I think it may affect humans more than others.' He put the phone back into his pocket. 'Do you forgive me?'

She grinned at him. 'Of course, I do. But no more lies between us, okay?'

Jack nodded. 'We need to get up the cliffs.'

Before she could reply, someone shouted at them.

'Yoo-hoo, little girl and rabbit, can you help me?'

Ella turned to see something which hadn't been there a minute ago, another strange sight in this strange land. A giant shark was sitting on a stone, brushing its teeth with a toothbrush as large as Ella's arm.

'That's something you don't see every day,' Jack said. 'What should we do?'

Ella moved towards the shark.

'Let's talk to it.'

It stopped brushing when they got there.

'Oh, little girl and big rabbit, can you help poor Sophia. I can't eat with these dirty teeth, and I need my toothpaste or my gnashers will fall out.'

A strong smell of fish hit Ella as she moved up to the shark, but not too close.

'We'd love to, Sophia, but we're on a mission, and we can't delay.'

Jack's daughter's ill health was playing on her mind. She had a new reason to get to Pandora as soon as possible.

'I know what you're up to and if you help me, I'll help you.'

Ella stared at her. 'How do you know about us?'

The shark's enormous choppers glistened in the sun.

'Everyone knows about the little girl and the rabbit on their way to fight the Empress.' Sophia started brushing again, talking and cleaning her teeth at the same time. 'But the little girl and the rabbit are no match for Pandora. So they need a weapon, and I know where you can get one.'

'Tell us about this weapon,' Jack said.

Sophia stopped brushing. 'There's a weapon which kills the gods, but it's hidden away, and only a few know where it is.'

'And you know where it is?' Ella said.

The shark held on to the brush in her arm-like fin and shook it at her.

'I do, little girl, and if you get me what I want, I'll tell you where the God Killer is.'

Ella glanced at Jack. 'What have we got to lose?'

'Nothing, I guess.'

Ella faced Sophia again. 'Where is this weapon?'

Sophia tilted her head up to the sky, just enough for Ella to notice how large her teeth were. And how much they needed a good clean, considering they were filled with bits of fish bones and seaweed.

She stepped away from the smell.

'The weapon is in the clouds?'

It didn't seem strange as she remembered the floating wolf head from before.

The shark's laugh sent debris from her teeth all over the sand, and Ella was glad she'd moved back.

'No, silly. Look higher.'

Ella did that, peering beyond the clouds until she saw something familiar hanging in the sky.

'The moon? The weapon is on the moon?'

'And my toothpaste. Lots of good things are on the moon.'

Jack shook his head. 'Even if this is true, how would we get there?'

'That's easy,' Sophia said. 'You just need to pay the toll to the cows on the cliffs. They have the rocket to take you there.'

Cows that take you to the moon. Why wasn't Ella surprised by that?

'Okay,' she said. 'We'll return later with your toothpaste.'

Then she set off for the cliffs with Jack by her side.

'Thank you, little girl. Be careful up there.'

'Do you believe any of that?' Jack said.

She shrugged as she trudged through the sand.

'Why not? And anyway, I've always wanted to go to the moon.'

Ella remembered reading the H G Wells book when she was younger, and only last year she'd watched a movie about it with her mother. She was thinking about that when they reached the steps at the bottom of the cliffs. They looked old and hardly used, with bits of them peeling away. There were rope handrails on either side, which were as frayed as Jack's nerves appeared to be as he put his hands on them.

'I don't like heights, Ella.'

'You'll be okay, Jack. I'll be behind you. Don't worry.'

'Perhaps you should go first. If I fall, I wouldn't want to take you with me.'

'No, you'll be fine.'

She'd ridden enough high rollercoasters not to be afraid of climbing, but the steps under her feet creaked a lot as she followed him up the side of the cliff.

He was cautious as he went, taking each step slowly as the wind increased the higher they got, swirling dust and sand around them until she let out a huge sneeze. She had to stop and cling on to the rope as her body shook.

Jack continued up, and so did she, seeing the top getting closer. She was glad when he got there and knew she was nearly done. He was reaching down to help her when a massive seagull flew at her face.

The bird squawked at her, screeching in Ella's ears as she twisted her head to the side so it missed her by inches. It hovered in the air as Jack dragged her to safety. She rolled from the edge and grabbed at her heart.

Then the bird spoke.

'She knows you're coming. She knows you're coming. And she's waiting.'

It flew away as Ella sat up. She was about to say something when a large cow approached them.

'Are you here for the trip to the moon?'

Ella put one hand on her chest and gathered her breath.

'If we can stay alive, then yes.'

The cow had huge brown eyes.

'The seagulls are terrible around here, always causing trouble. You won't have any of that on the moon.'

Jack helped Ella steady herself.

'You have a rocket to take us there?'

Ella found the cow's smile somewhat unnerving.

'We do. The Bullfather created the rocket to get us to and from the moon.' She glanced at Ella. 'We're safe up there.'

Ella returned the smile. 'Who is the Bullfather?'

'The Bullfather is our leader, a genius who keeps us all protected from those who want to enslave and harm us.'

The pigs live underground and the cows are on the moon. This all makes sense.

'Okay,' she said. 'Take us to this rocket.'

'It'd better be big,' Jack said under his breath.

And it was.

The cow took them fifty yards across the cliff and into the next field. Ella had watched TV programmes about rockets and NASA, but what she saw was nothing like that. About thirty feet tall and the same wide, a cigar-shaped metal cylinder was standing in the middle of the grass.

Jack stood next to her. 'It looks about as safe as that climb up the cliffs.'

The cow must have heard him. 'Oh, don't worry, dearie. We've never had an accident yet.'

Ella strode towards the machine. 'How many trips have you made?'

The cow chewed on a piece of grass.

'With this rocket? You're privileged to be aboard its maiden voyage.'

'Great,' Jack said.

The cow kept on chewing. 'My name is Laura, and I'll

be your guide and pilot on the trip today. Do you have the fare for the journey?'

Jack and Ella glanced at each other.

'How much does it cost?' Ella said.

'How much can you afford?' Laura replied.

Jack turned out his empty pockets.

'Nothing.'

Laura narrowed her eyes. 'Well, that is a pickle, isn't it?'

Ella thought on her feet. 'Maybe we can do the Bullfather a favour when we meet him.'

The cow considered the suggestion for a few seconds.

'Okay, that will do. Now, follow me.'

A ramp descended from the rocket, and Laura led them on board. As Ella stepped into the metallic entrance, she looked at her surroundings and wondered if she'd get back or not.

14   THE WHOLE OF THE MOON

They entered a large area, which looked much bigger than it did from the outside, and made Ella think of the TARDIS from *Dr Who*. Laura nodded towards the seats in the corner, and they strapped themselves in.

'Hold on to the sides, dearies. When we get out of the atmosphere, I'll bring the shutters down so you can have a magnificent view of space.'

Ella twitched a little against the straps pulled tight across her chest. It reminded her of the invisible chain Mary Lynne had used and she wondered how the magician was getting on with her new robot friends.

'What are you using for fuel?' Jack said to the cow.

Laura ambled to the far corner to sit over a circular shape on the floor.

'The Bullfather has programmed the rocket for everything: taking off, trajectory, and landing. All the pilot needs to do is provide the energy.'

Ella heard the floor moving underneath the cow and knew what was coming next. Gas seeped from Laura and into the hole as Ella placed one hand over her nose. She coughed as she spoke.

'How long will this take?'

'Oh, don't worry, dear. I ate a hearty meal today, and there'll be lots of gas to get us there in no time at all.'

Laura's stomach gurgled as the rocket moved underneath them. The sides trembled and the roof moaned as Ella's legs shook and that smell filled the room. She gripped her nose as the rust-bucket lifted from the ground and took them up. Everything wobbled and creaked, and she watched Jack grimace as he held on to his seatbelt.

Ella closed her eyes and tried to think of good things.

But she couldn't.

Her mind was full of what the shark had said about a weapon on the moon which could stop Pandora: the God Killer.

But I won't kill her. If we find this weapon, I'll use it only to scare Pandora, to prevent her from returning to Earth.

The thought of home made her wonder where they were heading. She turned to Jack.

'In your world, do you have a moon?'

He nodded. 'We do.'

'It's the same on Earth. So is this the same moon, or a different one?'

The cow must have heard what she'd said.

'The moon is a nexus point, dearie. It exists in all worlds, and sometimes beings can cross over on it at will.'

'Cool,' Ella said without really knowing what Laura meant.

Jack touched her arm. 'Perhaps we should get some rest. We haven't slept in ages.'

He was right and she closed her eyes.

'Don't worry, dearies,' Laura said, 'I'll wake you when we're close.'

Ella thought of the God Killer as the cow let out another massive burst of gas.

And the rocket sped them to the moon.

———

SHE DIDN'T KNOW how long she'd slept, but she felt a lot better when she woke. She rubbed at her face and heard Jack snoring. The cow also appeared to be sleeping as Ella undid her seatbelt. She went to stretch her legs, but couldn't reach them as her body floated out of her control.

Damn! I forgot about the gravity.

Or the lack of it. She lifted and banged her back against the roof.

'Ow.' A surge of pain rippled through her.

'I'm sorry, dearie, I should have warned you about that. You'll be fine soon when we land. You can pull yourself down using the grab handles around the sides. And I'll open the shutters for you to admire the view.'

She did that as Ella found the grips and lowered herself. Jack woke up as she did, and they peered out of the windows together.

'That's magnificent.'

Ella gazed at the planet below, recognising the familiar sight of Earth and wondering why she saw that and not Everywhere. Jack must have read her mind.

'I guess where we are, even in space, is part of this nexus Laura mentioned.'

Ella removed her phone and took a load of photos.

'Have you heard of this nexus before?'

He nodded. 'Lots of time during my travels through

Everywhere. The nexus joins the multiverse together and provides all the gateways between worlds, like the ones we came through.'

She continued to stare through the window, amazed at what she saw. She'd witnessed many marvellous things since following Pandora, but this sight was the one that took her breath away the most. The Earth looked like a blue marble with white swirls, dotted with brown, yellow, green and white colours. The blue part was water. The white swirls were clouds. The brown, yellow and green parts were land. And the white parts were ice and snow.

And she missed them all.

She raised her thumb in front of her and blotted out the Earth from her view.

'Okay, dearies, strap yourselves in. We're about to land.'

Ella followed the cow's instructions and eased her back into the metal of the rocket. A buzz of noise told her something was coming out of the ship's bottom and she assumed it was the legs.

The landing gear.

Laura stood and wiggled her backside.

'That's enough from me. Brace yourselves for the drop.'

Ella grabbed on to the side and waited. Jack was whistling some tune she didn't recognise.

If he doesn't like heights, what's he going to do on the moon?

The rocket thumped into the surface as she was considering that. Her seat lifted a little into her backside and she lurched forward, glad to be strapped in. The rocket rocked and rotated to the side, shaking her so much, she thought she was trapped inside a bowling ball rolling down an alley. Her stomach churned and she had to stop herself from throwing up.

She glanced at Jack to see his white fur shimmering and his eyes as wide as saucers. He gurgled something to her, but she couldn't understand what it was.

Yellow lights started flashing opposite her.

'The Cow has landed,' Laura shouted.

Ella took a deep breath and reached out for Jack, gripping on to his trembling paw. Sweat covered him and she felt a chill trickle down her spine.

'You'll be fine.'

Laura moved towards her. 'It won't be long now, dearie.'

Ella removed her seatbelt. 'Where are the spacesuits?'

The cow's eyes grew as big as her head. 'Spacesuits? What spacesuits?'

'For outside. We'll need them on the moon. It has no atmosphere.'

She remembered her mother mentioning that.

The cow bellowed out a hearty laugh, which made her udders tremble.

'Of course there's an atmosphere, dear. The cows wouldn't be living up here otherwise.'

Before Ella could react, the door opened and the ramp descended. Laura strolled down it while Ella held her breath.

How long can I keep this up?

Jack strode past her. 'She's right, Ella. I can smell the flowers.'

She relaxed her lungs and watched him step outside into the light. Ella hesitated for only a second before following him. She'd seen photos of astronauts on the moon, in their silver spacesuits, standing in the dust, surrounded by craters and the darkness of space.

What she stared at now was none of that.

The sky was a thick blue with pinpricks of stars glittering in the distance. The land wasn't grey, but a bushy, lush green from the mass of lawn covering it. Flowers were everywhere, and they smelt of lavender and roses. It was the most beautiful garden she'd ever seen.

And it was on the moon.

She stepped on to the grass. 'How is this possible?'

Laura strode towards her. 'You'll have to ask the Bullfather that. The mechanics of all this is beyond me.'

Ella nodded and turned to see Jack lying in the grass.

'This is magnificent. I might be in heaven.'

She sat next to him, running her fingers through the grass and feeling completely content.

'Do the people in your world believe in God?'

He sat up. 'Oh, yes, we have many religions and beliefs.' He leant closer to her. 'Though I don't know what they'd all think if they saw the things I have.' He glanced at the stars. 'Especially this.'

Laura strode over to them.

'You can eat the grass straight from the ground. It's tasty and very nutritious. Much better than that down below.'

Ella was hungry and tempted, but didn't. Jack did, gulping down a large handful and exclaiming how nice it was.

'I think I might stay here.'

Ella took hold of his arm. 'Don't forget why we're here. And remember Olive.'

Her name shook him out of his joy and he stood.

'You're right. Let's find this weapon and get back.'

She nodded. 'And the other thing.'

'The other thing?' he said.

Ella turned to Laura. 'We came here for some shark toothpaste. Do you have that on the moon?'

'Oh, yes, dear. Everything you could ever want is on the moon. I'll take you to the transporter.'

She trotted away and they followed, walking from the rocket and towards a building Ella hadn't noticed before. It looked like a small train station as the two of them continued to breathe in the purest of air.

'The moon for your world, Jack, is it anything like this?'

He shook his head. 'Definitely not. The first rabbits on the moon sent back photos of black space, grey earth, and what they called the magnificent desolation. And there was no air for breathing.'

'It's the same for our moon.' She watched Laura step through the door. 'I wonder if the Bullfather did all this.'

'He must be some genius scientist if he did.' They paused outside. 'Perhaps he's the one who created the weapon we want, the God Killer.'

'We'll ask him when we meet.'

Laura was waiting for them when they entered, standing in front of a lift.

'We're going underground.'

She stepped inside and they followed her into a metal box lit by bright lights. It descended immediately, with no warning, and Ella stumbled into the cow.

'I'm sorry,' she said when she straightened herself.

'Don't worry, dear. You're not the first to do that.'

Ella's guts bounced up and down like a ball on an elastic band as the lift kept on going before it stopped with a shudder.

'Are we going to meet the Bullfather?'

Laura didn't answer as the lift opened and they stepped into a vast space. Ella had seen a movie once where some evil genius had built an enormous base full of machines with scientists and soldiers trying to conquer the world.

This place was like that, apart from the fact there were no people, only cows.

And the Bullfather.

She guessed it was him as he stepped towards her. He was huge, towering over her and taller than Jack, probably eight foot tall. His legs were thicker than tree trunks, his hide a thick black matched by his eyes. Then she looked closer and saw the many scars on his skin. Ella didn't know how to respond, so she waited for him to talk.

'Welcome to the Bovination.'

His voice was deep and loud, so much so it hurt her head. She didn't know whether to bow or curtsey or just do nothing. Jack stepped in while she was trying to sort her brain out.

'Thank you, Bullfather. It's kind of you to have us here.'

'Yes,' Ella found her voice. 'Thank you very much. We came to get some shark toothpaste.'

She wondered if it sounded as silly out loud as it did in her head.

The Bullfather moved towards her and she shivered a little as his great snout got within inches of her face.

'Is that right? I thought you were here to kill a God.'

15 THE MOON IS BLUE

Fifteen minutes later, they were sitting at a table in another room, eating the best vegetable curry she'd tasted, and the first Jack had ever had.

'This is truly the food of the gods.'

Ella picked a piece of broccoli from her teeth.

'You don't have curry in your world?'

He shook his head. 'No, but you must give me the recipe to take home.'

She laughed. 'Don't ask me. I didn't cook it.'

'It's my special formula, brought all the way from our Earth, Ella Finn.'

The fork full of potato hovered in front of her lips.

'You're from my Earth?'

The Bullfather took up a vast space in the small room, which made him more imposing.

'I am. It's one reason why, even here, on this Moon of Everywhere, I'm still tuned into that place, especially the recent magical events of Pandora's return.'

'You know her, then?' Jack said.

'Only by reputation, until I sensed what was happening on that Earth and she visited me here.'

'What?'

Bits of curry dripped from Ella's lips and on to her leg. They were warm to the touch, but a chill was running across her skin.

Have we been tricked into coming to the moon? Is it all a trap?

The Bullfather must have read her mind.

'Don't worry, Ella. Unlike many others in Everywhere, I'm not working for Pandora. I've had my fill of tyrants.'

She wiped the food from her mouth.

'Animals can't talk on my world.'

'Are you sure?'

'I think so.'

'Perhaps I should tell you how I came to be here on this moon.'

She grabbed a glass of water from the table and settled into her chair.

'Yes, please do.'

'Animals can talk on our Earth, Ella.' He smiled at her. 'It's just that most humans can't understand us.' She was surprised at the sadness in his eyes. 'I was a purebred bull bought for breeding, the largest of my kind, purchased to service twenty-five to fifty cows during the breeding season. The humans put me in a pen with sturdy fencing, no chance of escape, but plenty of feed and water available. I hated it from the beginning, refusing to settle down and perform my duties. I tried to kick down the fence, but the barriers were too strong for me, even with my great height and physique. Many cows were there with me, but I either ignored them or threw myself against the wood, which constrained me, time and time again. I ached and bled, but it was no use. I was trapped.

'I'd shout at the humans to let me out, not knowing why they couldn't understand me, fighting against them as they tried, again and again, to get me to mate. After two weeks of unsuccessful attempts at bovine copulation, they chained me up in the corner of a fetid barn. Twice a day, one of them would visit me with an electrical prod, sending pain surging through my hide as punishment or incentive. I put up with it all, seeing the burns on my flesh as marks of my strength. I refused everything until the cow spoke to me.'

Ella's heart sank into the pit of her stomach.

'What did she say?'

'I saw the whites of the cow's eyes approach me in the fading light of the day; heard the sadness in her dispirited voice. "*If you don't breed, they'll kill you,*" she said.

'"Why?" I asked, confused by the world surrounding me.

'"*Because we're cattle. Do you know what that means?*" she replied.

'I shook my head and fought back the tears. I remembered nothing of my childhood, just a time spent on my own, provided with food and water by the humans. I didn't see any of my kind until I arrived on the farm.

'"*We're food for the humans, bred to provide sustenance for them. To live and die so they can live. You're here to make more cattle, to breed with us. If you do that, we'll all stay alive a little longer.*"

'"But we'll all die, eventually?" I said.

'"*Everything dies eventually, even the humans,*" she replied.

'So I did as the cow – Clara - asked and my hatred of the humans grew every time I bred. I dreamt of the time before my death when I'd inflict pain on them, kill at least one of them. It was all I lived for. Until I fell into Everywhere and my life changed.'

Ella gripped on to the fork so hard, her knuckles throbbed. She let go of it and placed it on the table.

'What happened then?'

'I met a cat called Blackstar and he talked about a revolution against the humans, of a war to wipe them out forever.'

Ella's throat turned into sandpaper.

'Is that why you're here on the moon, to work with Pandora to destroy all of humanity?'

It must have been a trap, after all.

The great bull shook his head.

'No. Some good people, both humans and animals, taught me valuable lessons. I abandoned Blackstar's plan on another world and travelled across Everywhere to find somewhere I could finally call home.'

'And this is it?' Jack said.

'I believe so. But I didn't get here straight away. I discovered a strange and magnificent thing as I journeyed through the multiverse: my intelligence grew with every new world I visited until I had the brain capacity to do many fantastic things, even inside this body.'

Ella bit into her lip. 'So you invented space travel and converted the moon into a habitable place?'

'No. The moon was like this when I arrived, and I got the idea for the rocket from a movie I saw once back on the farm.'

Jack whistled loudly. 'Still, it's impressive.'

Ella took another sip of water.

'What do you know about Pandora?'

The Bullfather stared at her.

'Probably less than you, Ella Finn, since she's your ancestor.'

The water chilled Ella's throat.

'How do you know this?'

'As I said earlier, somehow, through travelling across many parts of the multiverse, my brain power and my senses have become more heightened. I look at you and I see the same aura around your body she has. I recognise the same structure in your skin and bones. And you have the same Light flowing through you.'

Ella nearly spat the water all over the table.

'You know about Light and what it is?'

'As much as anyone, I suppose. It has different names across the many worlds, but Light defines who we are. Some beings have more of it and can use it to wield great power. Pandora is one of these, and she has the greatest power of all: the gift of creation.'

Ella rubbed at her throat.

'Are you working with her?'

'No. I refused her offer of a part in the destruction of humanity.' The Bullfather gazed at Ella. 'We can't let the mistakes of the few make us believe the majority are guilty of the same crimes.'

But Ella was consumed by guilt.

'Humans do terrible things to animals. Don't you want to stop that?'

He stepped towards her. 'Yes. But I think that has to come from humanity itself, don't you?'

She did. She absolutely believed that. Just like she knew she had to prevent Pandora anyway she could.

'Do you have a weapon I can use against her?'

'You mean the God Killer?'

'Yes.'

The silence cut through the air and seemed to last for an eternity.

'No. There's no such thing here.' Her heart sank. 'We are not in possession of the God Killer.' He peered deep into her. 'That is inside you, Ella Finn.'

Her eyes grew as large as his.

'What?'

Jack jumped up from his chair.

'I knew it. I knew it was you all along.' He ran to her. 'I told you, my friend. Now you know what you have to do.'

She pulled away from him.

'No, I can't. I'm not as strong as her. I'm not.'

She stood in front of them, turning her hands into fists. The blood rushing through her was hot like lava, and she was ready to explode.

'Strength comes in many forms, not just the physical. How did you feel when your parents disappeared?'

'I knew I'd find them.'

'Perhaps that's true, Ella, but you had more difficult times to contend with: travelling to the other end of the country to live with your aunt and uncle; having to deal with three cousins who hated you; being betrayed by your friend, and then discovering the truth about Pandora and her connection to you.'

She peered into the Bullfather's face.

'How do you know all these things?'

'Pandora told me. She's afraid of you. She tried to convince me you're a danger to all of us.'

The heat continued to rise inside her.

'She's a liar.'

'I know. I've spent most of my life around humans who lied to me, so it was easy to recognise it in her. It's also how I know you're the opposite of her.'

Ella's breathing returned to normal.

'I'm still not strong enough to do what needs doing.'

'Look at what you've done since you followed her across the realms, how you've dealt with everything thrown at you in Everywhere. You're stronger than you think, and that strength will only grow.'

Ella sat down and considered what she'd heard. It had been a wasted trip and she wanted to scream. Then she turned to Jack.

'What do we do now?'

He smiled at her. 'We get the shark toothpaste, return to the ground, and continue north.'

'No, there's something else we need first.' She looked at the Bullfather. 'We're looking for an item which heals the sick and dying. Do you have that here?'

It was a strange sight to see the bull shake his head.

'No, but I can tell you about someone who might have that information.'

Jack's eyes lit up and Ella finally felt good about something.

16 BEYOND THE SEA

The Bullfather instructed Laura to fly the rocket further up the coast and drop them off in an abandoned city. When she did, Ella peered through the window at the empty streets and uninhabited buildings.

'What is this place?'

'It was once the capital of a great nation, but many years ago, a virus ran through it and killed most humans. The only place of note now is where you need to be, just across the road from where we are.'

'The Empire of the Sea?' Jack said.

'Yes. That's where you'll find the person who has the knowledge you seek.'

Jack looked at Ella. 'What about the virus that wiped out most of the human population?'

'Don't worry. That died out after a few years. You'll be fine.'

Ella wasn't convinced, but would take the risk for Jack.

'How do we get inside this building?'

Laura used her nose to press the button to open the door and lower the ramp.

'The Bullfather knows the owner and called ahead. They're expecting you.'

They thanked her before stepping outside. Ella expected the city to stink of pollution and rotting flesh, but it was the exact opposite: nature had returned to the place with grass and flowers everywhere, making the streets smell like the countryside.

They left the rocket and headed across the road towards the biggest building they could see. Ella went first as they strode up the steps, with the Bullfather's words still ringing in her ears as she tried to stay focused on finding what Jack needed to save his daughter.

The door opened before they approached, an electronic lock slipping out of place as she stared at the cameras above their heads. They entered and walked down a long corridor, over a weathered carpet which had seen better days, and into a room large enough for a football pitch. The building was nearly as tall as it was wide, with a lavishly ornate beamed ceiling housing a magnificent chandelier. The walls were adorned with oriental silks and other exotic fabrics, while the floor was plush with a luxurious mahogany-coloured rug. Looking at it made Ella want to throw off her shoes and let her feet melt into its warm embrace.

Scattered around the place were several sofas, with the spaces in between inhabited by cushions of differing colours. At one end of the room stood a thick black working desk, on which there was a statue of a phoenix rising from the flames. From behind it strode an imposing figure of a man over six foot tall, with a physique which would have been at home in a heavyweight boxing ring.

'My name is Zachary Atlas: welcome to my abode.'

Ella couldn't say which was the most impressive, the fancy house or the vast beard covering most of Atlas's face.

'Thank you,' she said.

He sat opposite her, close enough for her to smell his cologne, which was sweet and sickly. His eyes were bright and wide, continually observing what was happening around him, flicking from side to side in unceasing motion. His nose was small and thin between chiselled cheekbones.

'How are things on the moon? Is the Bovination still going strong?'

Jack smiled at him. 'I'm thinking of retiring there.'

Atlas's laugh made his beard shimmer.

'You're the first humanoid talking rabbit I've met. You're quite impressive.'

'Thank you,' Jack said.

Atlas nodded before returning his attention to Ella.

'This isn't your Earth, is it?'

'No,' she said. 'I'm on my way back there, but the Bullfather said we should look at your collection first as there isn't anything like it in the multiverse.'

What he'd actually told them was not to tell Atlas why they were there under any circumstances.

'One of his possessions has the knowledge you want, but Atlas doesn't know it. It would be for the best if you can keep it that way.'

'The Bullfather is correct. I have to say, when I met him, I was blown away. I hadn't been in Everywhere for long, and he was the first intelligent talking animal I encountered. He was the one who inspired me to start my collection to save as many endangered creatures as I can. We humans have done our best to wipe out our species, but I couldn't let that happen to any others.'

Ella smiled at him. 'Well, we're keen to see it.'

'Yes,' he jumped out of his seat, 'let's get started.'

He led them to the back and through a large door. They

strode into a giant aquarium, the likes of which she'd never seen before. Her father had taken her to Sea World in the city when she was younger, and she'd hated it, being so close to all those aquatic creatures confined inside tiny cages of water when they should have been swimming in the great oceans of the planet. From the smallest, most exotic fish through to the largest whales, all of them appeared to be shedding watery tears to the young Ella. It had given her nightmares for months afterwards, and when her father brought a brightly coloured goldfish home in a bowl one day, all she could do was scream at him and run to her room.

What she saw when walking into Atlas's Empire of the Sea was much worse than her childhood experience. Numerous giant see-through prisons housed creatures who shouldn't have been anywhere near dry land. The place was as big as a large arena, with glass cages running around the insides like a giant inland waterway.

'This is one huge fishbowl.'

Jack sounded impressed. Ella grimaced at the thousands of exotic fish behind glass larger than the *Titanic*.

'It's the biggest collection of aquatic creatures in this world,' Atlas said proudly.

'Apart from what's in the sea,' Ella said.

She stared at what was beyond the massive school of fish. Separated into their liquid enclosures, were dolphins, sharks, squid, octopuses, whales, and many strange and unusual others she didn't recognise. The prison wall was thick and it was hard to understand what they were crying out for, but she got the gist of it: *we want to go home*.

Ella pushed her face against the cold glass, hoping to hide the tears she felt coming, peering at a baby whale, its pale skin making it appear malnourished and frail. Its eyes were large and wide, and she wanted to dive into them and tell it everything was going to be okay. But she knew it would be a lie.

'What's it like in the sea?' she heard it whisper.

'Isn't it marvellous we could breed them here?'

Atlas was oblivious to the pain and discomfort swimming through his underwater kingdom. Ella needed to help the poor creatures, but didn't know how. Her sadness cut through her in a great wave, injecting sorrow into every cell of her body. She thought of smashing her head through the glass and liberating all of them, even though she knew how foolish it would be.

'It must have taken you a long time to collect these,' Jack said.

'Yes, but I've saved the greatest part of my collection for last. You won't see anything like this anywhere in the multiverse.'

Ella put both hands on to the glass imprisoning the whales and whispered, 'I'm sorry,' before turning to face Atlas. 'Do you have a couple of mermaids imprisoned as well?'

It was taking all of her self-control to keep on top of her fury. She hated herself for it, but she knew they were there for one specific reason, and she couldn't let her anger ruin it.

His laugh was unconditional and wild, that of a man not used to having other humans around him. It made her wonder how he ran the place.

'No, something even better; look over here.'

Atlas continued laughing as he went to the far corner of the room. There was a giant cage there, not underwater, but covered by a large blanket. He skipped towards his secret possession, grinning like a court jester about to play his biggest practical joke. His face was manic as he stared straight at Ella.

'Are you ready to meet the world's oldest living creature?'

He waited for her response, but all she gave him was the angriest look she could muster, hoping the fire burning from her would leave a permanent scar on his heart.

Atlas grabbed hold of the cover, performed a mock flourish and bow, and then ripped it from the cage. Ella walked over to the metal prison and peered through the bars at the giant turtle sitting there: he was as big as a car. His eyes were closed, and she wondered if he was even alive.

'He's magnificent,' she said.

'I've had this fella for thirty years, but I believe he could be over two centuries old, making him the oldest living creature on the planet.'

Atlas's face beamed, pride and joy shining out of him like the rays of the sun. Inside Ella, it was as if an iceberg was sinking all of her hopes and dreams. She kept staring at the turtle, so motionless she thought he might be a waxwork. Then his wrinkled grey neck moved a little and she saw life in his eyes.

'I'm sorry for what they've done to you.'

She wanted to reach out and touch him, but stopped herself. She hated it when other people petted caged animals as if they were doing them a favour.

'Don't be,' he said. 'I'm safer here than in the real world.' His voice was like that of a grizzled old man who'd witnessed far too much heartache in a long life. 'And don't worry; that fool can't understand what I say.'

'Why are you safer in here?' Jack asked.

The turtle swivelled his legs inside his craggy shell, turning to face the rabbit.

'There are too many creatures out there who are after what's in my head, my friend. Atlas thinks I'm two hundred years old, but I've lived for over two thousand years. I know secrets from many worlds, and some people, including him, would do terrible things to have some of what I know.' His mouth appeared to move in slow motion, even though his words came out at normal speed. 'And you can call me Tommy, but it isn't my real name.'

Atlas stood to the side, observing them.

'Can you understand what he's saying?'

'No,' Ella said. 'But we'll keep trying.' She moved closer to Tommy so Atlas couldn't hear them. 'What secrets?'

'Well, if I told you, they wouldn't be secrets, would they?' The turtle chuckled as his head went backwards, his gaze falling on Jack. 'Did you know that pet-keeping by humans is only a recent phenomenon? We're just commodities to them, possessions to make them happy, but they'll kill us as quick as anything when it comes down to it. They love their material goods more than anything else. They would rather wear dead animal flesh on their bodies than let us roam free in the wild where we belong.' He gazed at Ella. 'This girl will betray you when you least expect it, Mr Rabbit, you mark my words.'

She was ready to shout at the giant turtle when she heard a click behind her. Ella turned to see the gun pointed at her head.

17 TURTLE BLUES

Ella's legs froze as she stared at the gun in Atlas's hand. 'Why are you doing this?'

He inched away from Tommy the turtle.

'I have to return home, and I need you for that.'

'Me, why?'

He waved the pistol at her to move closer to Jack.

'You have the power in you, child, to free me from this place. If you do that, I'll let you and the rabbit live.'

Jack glared at him. 'I thought you enjoyed living inside your sea prison?'

Atlas's hand wavered as he laughed, with the gun trembling near Ella's face.

'Oh, it was wonderful for the first ten years, but it soon becomes tedious when you're the only human here, and there's nobody to talk to.' A mixture of anger and fear dripped from his eyes. 'And it's worse when I know the fish are talking to each other, and I can't understand a word.' He glared at Tommy. 'And that turtle has thousands of secrets that would keep me entertained for the rest of my life if only I could comprehend him.' He moved closer to Ella.

'This is how I recognise you have great power inside you, child, because I know you can understand what they're all saying.'

She ignored the gun aimed at her head.

'Why don't you leave here? There are plenty of other places in Everywhere where you can go.'

He slammed his free palm into Tommy's watery prison.

'No, they're all as bad as this monstrosity. I want to return to my world, to be with my people again.'

Against her better judgment, Ella felt sorry for him.

'You don't know where it is, do you?'

Atlas removed his hand from the glass and wiped the sweat from his forehead.

'No, I don't. I fell into this terrible place with no idea how to get out. But you, child, with the power inside you, you can send me home.' He jerked the gun away from her and pointed it at Jack. 'Otherwise, I'll kill you both, starting with the rabbit.'

Ella remembered a time at her old school when a teacher had a breakdown and collapsed in class while all the kids stared at him in astonishment. Zachary Atlas and his trembling pistol reminded her of that moment.

'You didn't collect these sea creatures here, did you, Mr Atlas?'

His face suddenly resembled the skin of the giant turtle he kept imprisoned.

'No. I fell down a hole and woke up in Everywhere. I travelled through many lands, trying to find my way home, but with no luck. Most places were terrible and dangerous until I found this city. There's plenty of food and water here, but no people. I didn't mind at first, especially when I stumbled into this aquarium and its automated system.'

Jack glanced above them. 'Machines run everything here?'

Atlas nodded. 'Yes, I don't have to do a thing. Generators supply the power, while there's a mechanical process that changes and cleans the water and makes sure every living creature is fed.' He relaxed his grip on the gun. 'Including me.'

'I can't help you,' Ella said. 'If I could do anything, I'd release each creature here back into the oceans of the world.'

Even as she thought of a plan to get away from him, she understood it meant leaving all the sea creatures behind, and it pained her heart.

His face flushed red as his hand shook.

'You lie, child. Years ago, the Bullfather passed through here, through this city, and he was the only animal I could understand. I wanted to keep him with me, but recognised it was impossible because he was so strong. So I struck up a friendship instead, brought him into my confidence, and we set up a communication system between here and the moon. He realised I needed to see humans again, and when he told me about you, I was overjoyed.' Atlas waved the gun at her head. 'Because I'd heard of you, Ella Finn, and knew you'd be my way out of this hell and a return home.'

'She can't help you, Atlas, but I can.'

For a second, Ella didn't realise where the voice had come from, until she turned to see Tommy with his face pushed up against the glass.

Atlas dropped to his knees and gazed at the turtle.

'I can hear you.' But he still pointed the pistol at Ella. 'Or have I finally gone mad?'

'You're as sane as me, Zachary,' Tommy said. 'And if

you let the girl and the rabbit go, I'll give you what you want.'

Atlas stood. 'How can I understand you after all this time?'

'All I had to do was change my tone for your human ears and brain to hear me. It's the same with all the other sea creatures here. I can get them to do that if it's intelligent conversation you require.' The turtle glanced at Ella. 'Or, if you prefer, I'll give you directions on how to return home. But you'll have to help me and the others as well as releasing Ella and her rabbit.'

Ella watched Atlas's hand shake as he seemed to consider Tommy's words. Then he spoke to the turtle.

'How old are you?'

Tommy appeared to shrug. 'Over two thousand years.'

Atlas's eyes lit up on hearing that. 'Have you travelled across different worlds?'

'Many times,' the turtle replied.

Atlas stumbled towards Tommy and leant against the glass.

'I could learn so much from you, and then go home with all that knowledge.'

'Yes, you could,' Tommy said. 'As long as you do as I ask.'

'What do you want?' Atlas said.

'Let the girl and the rabbit go, and then I'll tell you how to release everyone back into the sea.'

Atlas tapped on to the glass with the gun.

'Everyone apart from you. You'll stay with me.'

'Yes, Zachary. I'll tell you all the secrets of the multi-verse.' He glanced at Ella. 'So, do we have a deal?'

Atlas stood up straight and put the pistol into his jacket pocket.

'If you had a hand to shake, my friend, I would, but yes, we have a deal.'

'Good,' Tommy said. 'Now give us some privacy. I have something to say to the girl before she leaves.'

Ella saw the suspicion thick in Atlas's face, but he did as requested, giving her a mock bow before he left the room.

'Farewell, Ella Finn, until we meet again.'

'Not if we see you first,' Jack said as Atlas went through the door.

Ella stepped towards the turtle in his prison.

'I thought you hated humans. Why would you help me?'

'Who said I did this for you? Perhaps I did it for the rabbit.'

Jack pressed his paw against the glass.

'Well, thank you for that, but we have to go now.'

'Indeed you do,' Tommy said, 'but do you know in which direction?'

Ella's eyes lit up. 'Do you know where the healing cloth is to save Jack's daughter?'

The turtle shook his head. 'There is no such thing, child. Even in Everywhere, that's only a myth. But I'll tell you where to find Pandora.'

The news she couldn't save Jack's child left her frozen against the glass, unable to process what else he'd said. Jack helped her up and spoke to the turtle.

'Where is she?'

'Head north until you can go no further,' Tommy said. 'That's where you'll find her.'

Ella steadied her breathing. 'What will you do with Atlas? How will you get everyone safely to the sea?'

'Don't worry about us, Ella. I know how to handle him, and I'll keep all of us safe.' He inched away from the glass.

'Go through the door opposite the garage which exits this building. Then travel as fast as you can because you have little time.'

Before she could reply, Tommy disappeared into the water and left them there. Then Ella turned away and followed the turtle's advice, not knowing what to say to Jack about their failed attempt at finding the only thing to save his child.

They were silent as they stepped into the garage, where something caught Ella's attention. She put her hand on Jack's arm.

'Have you ridden a bike before?'

He climbed on to the biggest one and adjusted the seat.

'I'll have you know I was the district road race champion for four straight years before I got married.'

There were only three children's bikes for her to pick from, and she took the one painted bright purple.

'But these aren't road bikes; they're mountain bikes.'

Jack pressed his feet into the ground and grinned at her.

'It's all the same. The bigger question is, how do we get them out of here?'

He lifted his arm to point at the garage door in front of them.

Ella settled on to her bike and pedalled.

'I'm sure there's a button or something here.'

And she was right, finding a big red release switch at the side. The door whistled and creaked as it opened, and they cycled out. It was dark, with only the moonlight guiding them along the roads strewn with abandoned cars and bits of rubbish. She switched her bike lights on and led the way.

Jack pedalled next to her. 'I'm glad you know where north is.'

She glanced up. 'It's easy using the sky.'

The moon was hanging there like a giant balloon, and she wondered how the cows were doing and sang a nursery rhyme she hadn't heard in a long time.

'Hey, diddle, diddle, the cat and the fiddle,

'The cow jumped over the moon.

'The little dog laughed to see such fun,

'And the dish ran away with the spoon.'

'I know that one,' Jack said.

They sang it together, riding through the silence of the city towards their unknown destination, while all the time, Ella thought of those poor creatures she'd left behind in the Atlas mansion.

They'd never see the sea again.

Will I ever get home?

Fields of long grass surrounded them, and it smelt of fresh strawberries. They were cycling through the eerie quiet when a strange hum drifted through the air. They had ridden past a derelict church and graveyard before Ella saw the shimmer filling the whole of the sky. They stopped a few feet from it. The hairs on Jack's face trembled in the moonlight.

Ella shielded her eyes from the glare.

'Is that what I think it is?'

Jack nodded. 'Yes, that's a gateway in the multiverse. We should have seen a lot more of them on our travels.'

'As doorways between the lands?'

She continued to gaze at the golden gleam.

'They were the only way to cross between the worlds, but then something changed, and the gateways blurred into nothing or transformed into much smaller spaces.'

'Like holes to fall down?'

He laughed, 'Exactly,' though by the look on his face, she guessed it was no laughing matter. 'We should have stepped through one for each place we've visited.'

Ella gripped on to the handlebars.

'Hopefully, we won't have to go through any more after this. The end of Everywhere might be on the other side of this gateway.'

They stared at each other for five seconds. Then they rode through the shimmer.

Tiny shivers of electricity ran along her arm as they went through the light. Her stomach twisted one way and the other as she entered the gateway, one hand on the bike as the other reached for her throat. The back of her mouth tingled as if she'd drunk a pint of Coke in one go, with bubbles bouncing everywhere inside her.

Then the shimmer disappeared and she smelt the sea. They stopped just in time before cycling over the edge of a cliff.

Jack was next to her with hair standing on end, making his head look like a toilet brush.

'We're back at the seaside.'

Ella turned to the left to see the sand and the coast below them. The air was full of the smell of saltwater, and seagulls hovered in the sky. It was still dark, but not as bad as where they'd just come from.

'I think it's the early morning.'

It felt like the time when people should be heading for work, and the aroma of fresh flowers lingered around them. But, apart from the birds and them, there was no other living thing there.

Jack pointed to the small town in the distance.

'I guess we're going through there.'

She nodded, staring at the houses and buildings which were close by. It reminded her of the village where she'd lived with her aunt and cousins and abandoned her parents when she'd followed Pandora into a new world.

Perhaps I'm back.

She scanned the beach at her side, looking for a familiar landmark to confirm what she thought. And then she found it.

'The pier!'

'Are you okay, Ella?'

She clutched at her chest. 'I think I'm back in my world, Jack.'

'Are you sure?'

She slapped her hand on the bike, unable to contain her excitement.

'Yes. The buildings look the same, and the pier is there as well.' She pointed at it and turned to glance behind them. The shimmering gateway had vanished, replaced by the steelworks she knew had closed down years ago.

'Yes, it all seems the same.'

Past the pier would be more cliffs and the old farm-house where she'd left Billy. And her mum and dad.

Jack put his hand on her arm.

'But if we're still inside Everywhere, Ella, then Pandora might be here.'

He was right and a shiver ran through her. It wasn't cold in the early morning, but a chill gripped on to her bones and wouldn't let go. She had to move.

'Come on. Let's find out.'

They cycled towards the houses, followed by a group of seagulls overhead, travelling over the cliffs and down on to the path which ran parallel to the railway tracks. She expected to see a few people going to work or school, but there was nobody.

They stopped in the middle of the local allotments.

'Is it always this quiet?' Jack said.

Ella smelt the air and stared at a group of chickens peering at her through a fence.

'No. Saltburn is a small place, but there should be people here now.'

They set off again and reached the street in ten minutes. Ella stopped outside the shops, staring at the butcher's and remembering how much she'd hated walking past there and its smell of dead animals.

Then there were the happy times in the local bookshop, rummaging through the shelves for something to transport her to other worlds.

And look at me now.

She remembered going to the chocolatier and buying sweets with the little pocket money her aunt gave her, stuffing chocolates and toffees into her face to forget what had happened to her parents.

Pandora took them from me, but then I found them again. And then I abandoned them.

Her memories drifted away when she saw Jack's reflection in the glass.

'Is this where you lived, Ella?'

She glanced at the town clock ahead of them, staring as it struck eight in the morning.

'Yes. Most of these shops should be open by now, with cars and buses on the road.'

And the people? Where were they? Had Pandora got there before her and taken her revenge like she said she would?

'Where's your home, Ella?'

She ignored the ache in her bones to look at him.

'It was never my home, Jack, just the place where the police left me after my mum and dad disappeared.'

'But they returned, you said, so they should still be here, somewhere.'

'Yes, they returned, but I abandoned them, left them behind while I went chasing after Pandora with no idea what I'd do when I caught up with her.'

Ella jumped off the bicycle and threw it to the ground. The metal rattled across the concrete and echoed around the square. They'd reached the end of the world, after all.

Jack got off his bike, picked hers up, and leant them against the front of a shop.

'We don't know what's happened here, Ella. Let's not give up yet.'

She dug her nails into her palm.

'I'm not giving up. Whatever Pandora has done here, I'll make her suffer for it.'

And if she's harmed Mum or Dad or Billy, she'll pay dearly. Then I will be the God Killer.

For the first time since she'd given new life to the land and the lake in the cat community, she felt the Light flowing through her. Energy seeped through her blood and bones as if she'd plugged herself into an electrical socket. She peered into her hands, amazed to see the golden glow coming from her palm and fingers.

Jack saw it too.

'Is that your Light?'

She nodded. 'Yes, I think so. It's not like it was when I was connected to Pandora before, but it's increasing inside me.'

She was growing up, Ella understood that, not only physically, but emotionally as well. Her travels through Everywhere had changed her. She was quicker in mind and body.

Ella got out her phone to check the time, seeing it hadn't

gone beyond one hour. But she knew time moved differently outside of her world, so what if a few days in Everywhere were months or years here, back home? Decades may have passed, and everyone she knew might be no more. There could have been a war, or the climate could have finally given up against the pollution.

It could be hundreds of years since I left.

'Do you want to look for your parents?'

She did, and she didn't. What if she found them and they were dead? What if they died decades ago?

As she thought about what to do, the wind blew a newspaper towards her. She grabbed it and checked the date.

It's only a week since I left!

Ella showed Jack the paper. 'I feel old, but I'm not!'

She threw her hands in the air while he scrutinised the paper. Then she came back to Earth when she saw the town clock and remembered where they were. She took a deep breath and climbed on to the bike. She had to see if her parents and Billy were there. She nodded at Jack, ready to set off when she heard someone singing.

At least, she thought it was singing.

Jack dropped the paper to the ground. 'Where's that coming from?'

Ella peered above the clock and towards the train station. Down past there were the beach and the pier, the spot where she'd made friends with Billy and Dora.

Dora. The girl who'd pretended to be her friend.

Dora, who was Pandora.

'It's on the other side of the supermarket.'

'Should we see what it is?' Jack said.

'We have to.'

Ella pedalled as hard as she could, not worried about any traffic. They went under the archway and past the supermarket's metal shutters, following the sound of what she thought was a woman singing. Yet, she didn't recognise what the language was. She'd taken French and Spanish classes at school and knew it wasn't those.

Jack rode next to her as they reached the street.

'Do you know what she's singing?'

She shook her head as she pedalled.

'No.'

But whatever it was, Ella thought it was beautiful and felt the voice pulling at her heart.

The beach came into view as they moved from the houses and towards the pier. She squeezed on the brakes, ready for the tight corners that wound along like a snake, then hitting them fully as she saw what was in front of her. Jack did the same, but his wheel turned into her and he went face first over the handlebars and into the obstruction.

Ella threw her bike on to the road and ran to him.

'Jack!'

She bent her legs and reached down, expecting the worst when she flipped him over, ready for blood and a cracked head. But all he did was smile at her.

'Well, that was exciting.'

Ella lifted him and saw what he'd landed on and recognised the obstruction.

'Clothes. It's just a bunch of clothes.'

She ran her hand through the trousers, shirts, coats and jackets. She picked a few of them up and noticed they were all for adults. The singing had stopped as Jack shook the dust from his legs.

'Why would someone dump these in the middle of the road?'

Ella twisted her head and looked far and wide, searching for any other living thing. Even the seagulls had disappeared. She stared at the pier and the shops opposite it, the fish restaurant and the arcades, the surf shop and the little huts the tourists rented.

Is this my town?

It had to be. Apart from the lack of people, everywhere looked the same.

'Perhaps you should check the clothes, Ella, see if there's anything in them you might recognise.'

'The only adults I know here are my aunt and uncle and a few teachers.'

And the parents I left behind.

She thought about it while she glanced over the road at the clifftops, knowing her mum and dad should be in one of the houses there.

If they stayed where I left them.

It didn't matter. She had to look.

Ella grabbed her bike, ready to ride down the bank, go across the seafront, and then up the opposite hill until she reached the top and turned into the former fishermen's houses. It would be tough on the legs and the back, but she readied herself for it.

Then the sounds came again, but not singing this time; a long howling wail.

Jack put his paws over his head. 'What is that?'

She didn't know. Ella had heard nothing like it before, but it wasn't painful to her as it appeared to be to him. She checked the bike was okay and pointed it down the bank.

'Can you ride, Jack?'

He removed his hands from his ears.

'Yes, it's just irritating me now. Where are we going?'

'My aunt and uncle's house is up there.'

'Great. Maybe the height will dull that terrible sound.'

As she was about to agree with him, it stopped. He shook his head. 'Thank God for that.'

She couldn't help herself and smiled. Then she saw the movement coming towards them.

'The birds are back.'

Jack pointed up. 'That's not seagulls, Ella.'

The darkness in the air shimmered and swirled as it approached them, moving through the sky like a worm wriggling across the sand. It was too dark to see what it was until it reached the rays of the morning sun, and its head appeared. The teeth came first, sticking out like a tiger's, ready to bite her face off.

But this was no tiger.

It *was* a worm, a giant flying one with tiger's teeth about to devour her.

And then that horrible sound came again.

19 THE STORM

'Ride!' Ella shouted as she let the cycle go down the bank with the brakes off. The tyres screeched as she came to the first bend, turning the handlebars to the side so the bike twisted around it.

She didn't look back as the terrible noise followed her all the way, hanging over her head like a blanket ready to smother her. As she reached the second turn, Jack sped to her side with a paw over one ear and the other gripping on to the handlebars. They were approaching the last turn together when the giant flying worm swooped down and knocked them off their bikes.

Ella fell to the left, her leg hitting concrete as the bike rolled over her. She didn't see what happened to Jack, scrambling across the pavement as the worm came again. Sweat blurred her eyes, but she still saw the fangs coming at her, its vast gaping jaw spitting out venom that smelt like an unflushed toilet. Its breath was hot and wet as the teeth reached for her. She grabbed a handful of dirt from her side and threw it into the beast's face. It screamed and howled as she tumbled over.

She bumped into the bottom of a fishing boat and used it to drag herself up. The worm had disappeared, and so had her friend.

'Jack, where are you?' The silence sent a shiver down her spine, complementing the ache in her leg and hip. She shouted again. 'Jack?'

'Ellllaa,' he replied from above her.

Ella twisted her head, seeing the movement coming out of the clouds and straight towards her, ducking before his dangling legs hit her. Ella bumped into the boat, shocked to see the worm carrying Jack in its massive jaw. The worm's teeth were biting into his jacket and she hoped they hadn't gone into his body. The beast rose before twisting around to come back at her. She had to think quickly if she was to free Jack without getting him hurt. It dived for her again, howling and screeching as it held on to the jacket.

She waited this time.

And waited.

Turning two seconds into an eternity.

Until the last minute, when she swivelled and threw her arms around Jack's legs. She knew she weighed little, but hoped it would be enough to pull Jack from the jaws of the fiend.

It wasn't. It kept rising even as she dragged on her friend.

The worm flew out towards the sea.

'Let go, Ella,' Jack shouted. 'Leave me.'

She had to, but couldn't. She'd left Billy and her mum and dad behind, and now something must have happened to them in this terrible place.

I'm not leaving Jack.

She was repeating that in her head when the arrows whizzed past her and into the belly of the beast. The tips thudded into its chest and cut into its guts, the creature screaming as it let Jack go and they hurtled towards the water below.

Ella hit the waves, clinging on to Jack's legs, plunging into the sea and sinking below the surface. She let go of him as the inky darkness swallowed her whole. Saltwater rushed into her eyes and nose before filling her mouth. Her hands grasped at anything, only finding liquid that melted through her fingers.

Then she clutched at her throat instead, trying to breathe, but it was impossible while the ocean filled her lungs. Her legs kicked against the sea as a furry paw reached down and dragged her out of the water.

Jack laid her on the wet sand and peered into her eyes.

'Ella, can you hear me?'

His face was fuzzy in her eyesight as she coughed a great splurge of water over her body. He put one arm under Ella to lift her as she spewed out the sea again. After two more goes, she could breathe properly, but it felt as if someone had stuck a lead pipe into her lungs while jumping on her chest.

She was sitting up and rubbing at her eyes by the time she realised the flying worm was lying dead next to her, its body riddled with arrows.

Ella looked at Jack.

'Thanks.'

'I only did the simple part once we hit the sea.' He pointed to something behind her. 'They did the hard bit.'

Her ribs throbbed as she turned to see what he meant, surprised by a bunch of kids with bows in their hands.

And she recognised the boy at the front.

'Billy!'

She forced her aching body up and staggered towards

Billy Pudding, throwing her arms around him before he could react. Water dripped from every part of her as she felt the tension in him. Ella let go and gazed at the friend she'd left behind.

'There's no need to thank me. We all hate the earworms.'

She looked from him to the others, not recognising any of them, shocked to see them dressed in rags like Victorian street urchins.

'Billy, it's me, Ella. Ella Finn.'

Confusion filled his eyes. 'I don't know you, kid. Do you live around here?'

Ella's heart thumped against her chest at a thousand beats a minute. She struggled to breathe as she pointed to the row of houses on the cliffs.

'My aunt and uncle live on the farm up there.'

And they made me stay in the barn.

Not that she'd complained since it got her out of the house and away from her horrible cousins.

Billy and all the group eyed her suspiciously.

'The Twist Farm? You live up there?'

She nodded. 'I did.'

As one, they aimed their bows at her.

'That's where the earworms come from. And where *she* lives?'

Jack stood side by side with Ella.

'She?'

'She who controls the monsters, who took all the adults away.'

Ella ignored the boy's distrust, knowing now he wasn't the Billy Pudding she knew.

He looks like my friend, but it's not him. This isn't the same town I left. It's a different world.

Relief swept through her as it meant her parents and her Billy were safely back home.

'Have you seen this woman?' Jack said.

The fake Billy shook his head. 'No. We've only heard her voice. And seen what she does to the grown-ups.'

'What's that?' Ella said.

He pointed to the bunch of clothes in the middle of the road.

'When they hear her singing, that's what happens to them. I saw it with my own eyes, had to watch my ma turn into nothing.'

He wasn't her Billy, but her heart still sagged when she heard his words.

'But it doesn't do that to you and the other kids?'

'Yeah, that's why she sends the earworms after us.'

'When did this start?' Jack said.

'About ten days ago.'

Jack turned to Ella. 'Around the time you followed Pandora through the portal.'

'Did that cause the terrible things to happen here?'

She didn't want to believe it. It was she who'd forced Pandora to flee to Everywhere.

But I had no choice. And Pandora thought she was going straight to her realm.

Yet something went wrong.

'It might have. This place isn't your town but a duplicate with some changes.'

'Like me not being here?'

'Yes. And I don't think it's a coincidence we arrived here.'

'Why not?'

'Somehow, Pandora changed how Everywhere works when she stepped from your world into it. I guess she thought she was returning to the realm where humans imprisoned her, but it went wrong and she ended up in Everywhere. Do you remember what I told you about Everywhere, that it's like a corridor running through the multiverse with doors you could travel through from one world to another?'

She nodded. 'Yes, it's the theory of parallel worlds.'

'It's no theory, Ella; it's real. You know that now.'

'Of course,' she said.

'Well, I think Pandora, with all her power, with this Light burning inside her, somehow changed Everywhere. Now there are sections of realms not separated by shimmering gateways, but all merging into one place.'

He stopped to catch his breath, and she considered what he'd said.

'I think you're right, Jack, and what she did weakened her, which is why she's consumed energy from places like the cat community.'

He nodded. 'And all the time she's been trying to get back to the world which was once her prison. I believe the next time we go through a gateway will be the last.'

'Because it will be the end of Everywhere?'

'Yes, and that's where Pandora is.'

'And where we might find the healing power for your daughter.'

She still held on to that dream, regardless of what Tommy had said.

'Perhaps.' Great bags had formed in the fur below his eyes. 'We should locate the gateway now, Ella, before any of those worms return.'

She looked at Billy and his gang.

'We can't leave them like this, Jack. We need to go to the farm and see what's there.'

Maybe her aunt and uncle were still there.

He glanced over at the bank and the houses atop the cliffs.

'It might be best if we walk up. We don't want to get caught on the bikes riding uphill if one of those worms comes for us again.'

'Okay. It shouldn't take more than five minutes to get there.'

Billy offered her his bow and arrows.

'If you're going up there, you better have these.'

She shook her head. 'Thanks, Billy, but by the time I've sorted out how that works, the worm will probably have bitten my face off.'

Ella grabbed him instead, hugged him, and then let go. His face had turned red, and she smiled at the sight.

Jack waved at their saviours. 'Thanks again, kids, for saving us.'

Ella and Jack marched side by side as the sun bathed them in warmth and light. He spoke to her as they went.

'Are you disappointed this isn't your world?'

'No.' She thought she would have been. 'At least my parents and Billy are safe back there.'

The bruise on her hip ached as she strode up the road.

'What are we going to do when we reach the top?' Jack said.

'Find who is in control of the worms and make them stop.'

'And how will we do that?'

'I'll think of something.'

'What if it's Pandora?'

Ella stared across the sand and into the sea, watching the sun rising above the water.

'I hope it is. At least here, she won't have her army of

Elementals, just those monsters, and if a bunch of kids with homemade bows and arrows can take one of them out, we should be okay.'

'Because you're the God Killer?'

She peered into the palms of her hands.

'Because I'm the God Killer.'

But am I a killer?

20 SONG TO THE SIREN

They continued going up, past her aunt's favourite pub, until they reached the end of the road, pausing at the path leading to the row of old fishermen's houses. Then she saw the farmhouse and barn belonging to her relatives, the Twists.

Ella steadied her nerves as they headed towards the house. She thought the grass had grown long since she was last there, before reminding herself she'd never walked this route before. Her legs ached as she kept going, stopping fifty yards before the front of the house when she saw the lights inside.

Jack pointed to the building opposite the farmhouse.

'Is that the duplicate of the barn you told me about?'

'Yes, the one where my uncle made me sleep.'

And where I left my animal friend, Ratter.

'Are we going to walk straight inside?'

She was about to reply when the space at the cliff edge trembled and moved as if it was water in the air. They stood there and watched it vibrate for thirty seconds before it steadied into a familiar shimmering shape.

'That's the gateway to the next world,' Jack said.

Ella walked towards it, stopping at the edge before she tumbled below. The gateway had settled down, but it was two feet from the top of the cliff, and they'd have to jump out to make it. She reached out and watched her fingers disappear inside as her legs clung to dirt.

'It feels like electricity in there.'

Jack put his fingers on her shoulder to steady Ella on the ground.

'We could leave now. Pandora must be on the other side.'

It was tempting. All it would take would be one leap of faith. But she pulled her hand back.

'No. I want to see what's inside the house.'

She turned and marched towards the door. Jack ran to keep up with her.

'No plan?'

Ella grinned. 'Of course not.'

She pushed the unlocked door open and stepped inside. The entrance was the same as the Twist home in her world. Coats hung on the wall, shoes lay on the floor, and her cousin's phone sat on the table under the mirror. It was strange for her to see it, considering it was her cousins stealing her mobile that had started her adventures with myths, legends and other worlds.

Her hand hovered over the screen, wondering if there were messages on it about her or photographs of her parents. She stopped herself as she looked into the mirror, not recognising who stared back.

Is that me, or just a different version of who I was?

She was standing transfixed in front of the reflection when it spoke to her.

'*Everyone changes as they get older, Ella. It's called growing up. You can't stay a child forever.*'

She lifted a hand to her cheek.

But what if I could?

The idea of it ran through her skull like an insect scuttling in the dark. It was nibbling away at her brain as Jack shook her back into reality.

'There's someone in the kitchen, Ella.'

Her head throbbed as she stared at the door, listening to the sound of pots and pans being moved around. She didn't hesitate and pushed the door open.

'Well, you took a fine time getting here.' The woman was gutting a fish on the counter, the knife in her hand covered in blood. 'Do you eat fish, Ella?'

'I'm vegetarian.'

The woman shook her long, dark hair so it fell on to her shoulders.

'Yes, I'd heard that, but I thought your journey here might have changed you.'

Ella glanced around the room to make sure the woman was on her own. It looked no different to the one she was used to in her world, apart from the large harp standing near the window. That was new.

'Who are you?'

The woman put the knife down and wiped bloodied fingers across her white dress.

'I'm Thea.'

Thea held out her hand, but Ella didn't take it.

Jack moved forward. 'Are you responsible for that monstrous worm that attacked us?'

Thea nodded. 'I'm sorry about that. They can get very testy when they haven't eaten for a while.'

Ella gritted her teeth. 'What are you?'

Thea laughed. 'Why, whatever do you mean, child?'

'Pandora sent you here, didn't she?'

She could see it in the strange woman's eyes.

'I cannot tell a lie. I do as the Empress bids me.'

'What did you do to the adults in this town?' Jack said.

Thea retrieved the blade. 'Even though I'm from the sea, I never eat fish.' She gazed at Ella. 'So I have to chew on something else.'

'I know what you are,' Ella said. 'You were the one singing that strange tune earlier.'

Thea waved the knife in the air and dropped blood on to the floor.

'I don't trust anyone who doesn't like music.' She stared at Jack. 'What about you, rabbit? Do they have song and dance in your world?'

Ella stepped towards the blade.

'Why are you here?'

Thea bit her lip. 'You know, you're not what I expected. How old are you, thirteen? I anticipated a scared little girl bumbling her way through the worlds without knowing what she was doing, but you, you're nothing like that.'

Ella repeated her question. 'Why are you here?'

Thea pointed the knife at Jack.

'Who wouldn't want to rule a world when given the opportunity?'

'But this isn't a world, only part of it,' Jack said.

Thea's eyes narrowed. 'Indeed. Do you know what I found when I got here and I swam out to the furthest point in the sea?' He shook his head. 'Nothing. It ends about three miles into the horizon, just solid water with no way past. I'm assuming it's the same with the land, but since I have to stay close to the ocean, I haven't looked.'

'There's a gateway outside this house.' Ella was hoping to tempt Thea from the town. 'You could use it to leave.'

Thea stuck one finger into the fish guts.

'It's risky, not knowing what's on the other side. If there's no water there, I'd be done for. And you know you can't go back through the same gateway. No, I'll stay here for a while, let those kids grow up a bit, and then feast on them.' She removed her finger from the fish and licked the blood off. 'You two can leave. I'm only here to distract you.'

Jack put his hand on Ella's arm.

'We should do as she says.'

Thea smiled. 'And I'd heard you were such a dumb bunny.'

Ella shook herself free. 'We're not leaving you here. I'll get the rest of the kids, and they'll deal with you using their bows and arrows.'

Thea continued to suck on her finger.

'Well, you had your chance.'

Then she sang.

Audible honey poured out of her mouth, her vocals consuming all of the air and filling Ella's head. It was the most beautiful thing she'd ever heard, more heart-warming than her mother's voice telling Ella how much she loved her, more joyous than her father's words of pride for his daughter.

But it had no effect on her.

Ella glared at Thea. 'You don't scare me with your siren song. I know it's only for adults.'

The siren stopped singing and smiled at her.

'Is that so, child? Let's see what happens when I alter my tone.'

Her vocal was loud this time and the hairs on Ella's arms stood on end underneath her clothes. She had the urge to pull them off and scratch her skin, to tear the flesh from her bones. Music came from nowhere, a hum like a guitar creating invisible nails grabbing at her heart. Then it ran through her bones and pounced on her brain, a heavy weight that forced her to crash to the ground.

Ella grabbed at her head, sticking fingers into her ears to stop the thunder in her skull, but it was impossible. The noise was already inside her, clawing and scratching at every inch of her. Electricity shot through her as she screamed.

The siren lowered her face towards Ella.

'It didn't have to be like this, child, but you're so stubborn. Remember these words as I crush your brain with my song.'

Thea opened her mouth and something beautiful came from it, but all Ella heard was the sound of her flesh boiling and the destruction of her bones. She was wondering how she'd been so stupid when the singing stopped and blood dripped on to her neck.

'Take my hand.' Jack stood over her.

She grabbed him and he pulled her up. There was ringing in her ears, but she was okay and could hear the blood gurgling from Thea's throat. She turned to see the siren sprawled on the floor with red pouring from her flesh. Somehow, she still spoke.

'How... how?'

Jack threw the bloodied fork on to the table.

'Your charms only work on humans. You must have forgotten about that.'

Ella rubbed at her throat while Thea clawed at hers. There was blood on both of them. Ella was trying to quieten the noise in her head when an awful howl erupted outside. She was running before Jack could stop her.

She nearly fell over the dead earworm when she got outside, only stopped by Jack pulling her back.

'Killing the siren must have destroyed her creatures,' he said.

Ella gazed out upon the wriggling deaths of those terrible monsters, wondering where they'd come from.

Did Pandora create them?

'Are you okay, Ella?'

She wiped Thea's blood from her throat.

'Have you killed before, Jack?'

'No. But I had to, to save you.' She peered deep into his eyes, unsure whether to believe him. The gateway shimmered near to them. 'We should leave now.'

She shook her head. 'If what she said was true, the siren, this isn't a proper world but just part of one transported into Everywhere. She mentioned there's a barrier in the sea, so there must be the same on land. Billy and the other kids will have nowhere to go.'

'We don't know this, Ella. The town could return to its world the same way it arrived here.'

'No. Somehow I know the truth. Pandora did this, either by accident or on purpose.'

'I agree, but that means only she can reverse what's happened. It's another reason we have to find her. And stop her.'

By killing her.

That's all she thought about as they went to the gateway shimmering in the air above the sea and certain death below.

And then they jumped.

21 MOTION SICKNESS

They landed not on the sand or in the sea, but in the middle of a bright ginger path. When Ella's hands touched the stones, she thought they'd fallen into a giant orange since the surface was so soft.

Jack stood first. 'It smells of carrots.' He helped her up. 'Which is always a good sign.'

'This is the road to the end of Everywhere, to the end of the world.'

He stared into the woods on both sides of them.

'How do you know that?'

She peered at her hands. 'I just do.'

'You're not there yet, child.' Ella jerked around to see a small pink elephant speaking to her. 'This is The Land of Make-Believe. The Orange Road leads to the Realm of the Empress, but we're on the periphery of it, the place where she leaves the things of no use to her.'

Ella smiled at the talking elephant.

'What's your name, Mr Elephant?'

The elephant shook its trunk at her.

'I'm a Ms, I'll have you know, and the name is Olly.'

'When you say the Empress, do you mean Pandora?'

'That's her. I only met her once, but that was enough.' The top of Olly's trunk shivered. 'She wasn't nice at all. If you're looking for her, and I'd advise against it, follow the Orange Road and you'll arrive at her palace in the City of Dreams.'

'City of Dreams?' Jack said.

'That's what she calls it because everything she dreams comes true.'

Ella looked into the trees where Olly had come from.

'Why are you pink?'

'I think she was drunk when she thought of me.'

Jack smirked. 'Where is this place?'

'Not far.'

Ella knelt to be at the same level as Olly.

'Can I ask you a personal question?'

Olly's cheeks wobbled as she spoke.

'Sure, kid. I haven't had a decent conversation in goodness knows how long.'

'How old are you?'

Her trunk trembled. 'I don't know.'

Ella continued. 'Do you remember being a child, having parents?'

'Now that you mention it, I can't say I do. I woke up one day in the woods, and I had all this stuff in my head, and that's about it.'

'And you knew Pandora created you and about her City of Dreams?'

'I did. It was all in my brain. I can even see a picture of her now.'

'What does this mean?' Jack said.

Ella shrugged. 'I'm not sure. She's up to something, but I don't know what.'

'She's waiting for you,' Olly said.

Ella put one hand on the elephant's hide, noticing how soft it was under her fingers.

'How do you know that?'

'I've met some of her other creations, and we all have that thought in our heads. Pandora is waiting for Ella.'

Jack dragged her away from the elephant.

'Do you not think she planned this all along to lure you here where she has an army of creatures? Perhaps we should go back.'

Ella glanced behind her. 'Go where? The gateway has disappeared. Even if this is a trap, we can only move forward now.' She put a hand on his arm. 'And we need to find the healing cloth for your daughter.'

If it exists.

He turned from her, but not before she noticed the tear in his eye. He wiped it away.

'I wish we had some transport to get there quicker.'

'I'll give you a lift,' the elephant said.

Jack and Ella glanced at each other before she spoke.

'Are you sure, Olly?'

'Yes, I'm stronger than I look, and you're just a slip of a girl with nothing on you. Plus, it will give me something exciting to do for a change.' She stared into the trees. 'It's so boring here.'

Ella let Jack climb up first before he helped her on to Olly's back. Then the elephant trundled down the road. Ella put her arms around Jack's waist.

'I guess this is the only way to travel to the end of the world.'

'The end of Everywhere might be the end of every-thing, Ella, including us.' The elephant marched on at a steady pace. 'Why do you think Pandora is creating new life?'

Ella stared at the silent trees as they went.

'She couldn't return to her realm, so perhaps she's forming new things to be her Elemental army.'

'To take them to your world?'

'Yes. But that's if she can return there. I don't even know how I'll get home.'

'I know, Ella. I've been thinking about how to get back to my family as well.'

'Are you okay up there?' Olly said.

'We're fine,' Ella replied. 'We're not hurting you, are we?'

The elephant giggled a curious sound which reminded Ella of a seaside laughing policeman. It also made Olly move her back slightly, so Ella had to grip tighter on to Jack's waist.

'No, my dear. It's quite enjoyable helping you like this.'

Ella checked her mobile as they travelled, seeing the time still hadn't moved beyond an hour. She thought again about how much time would have passed when she returned home.

If I get home.

She put the phone away and stared at her hand. She'd used Pandora's Light to cross over into Everywhere, and some of it was still in her; she could feel it. She'd used that Light to heal the land and lake in the cat community, which had drained her, but it was returning slowly. So she should be able to use it to get home.

Once she'd dealt with Pandora.

She still didn't know how she'd do that, telling herself she wouldn't be a killer. Then the elephant stopped walking.

'There's something ahead. We'll have to go around it.'

'Okay,' Jack said as Olly started moving again.

Ella twisted her head beyond Jack's back to see what was on the road, but it was the smell that reached her first: the stink of rotting flesh and flies in the air.

'Oh dear,' Olly said. 'This isn't good.'

She walked around the obstruction, stepping through the grass verge as Ella peered at the dozens of bodies covered in insects. They were large birds, like flamingos, but with human heads.

Jack shivered next to her. 'Something terrible happened here.'

Ella put one hand to her face as the elephant stepped back on to the Orange Road and continued. Nobody spoke until they exited the tees, coming out of the shade to find a lake on their left. The road wound its way alongside the water, and she realised what she'd thought was a large shadow covering it was something else.

'We walk into the valley of death,' Olly said as they stared at the dozens of bodies floating in the lake.

This time they had human form, but with fishes' heads. Ella didn't cover her eyes, preferring to remember the result of Pandora's meddling with nature.

'Do you think they were part of Pandora's army?' Jack said.

'They must be,' she replied.

But what happened to them, and are there any others?

She got her answer as they continued travelling. It was a mile before they found the next corpses, creatures which had been half horse and half dog. There were two more lots of the dead along the route, more examples of Pandora's experiments gone wrong. Bears with monkeys' heads, and then, finally, the one which made Jack get off the elephant for a closer look. She didn't want to, but Ella did the same, peering at more than a dozen bodies.

Six-foot rabbits with shark heads.

Jack bent his legs to touch the fur of one of them.

'Why is she doing this?'

Ella put a hand on his shoulder.

'Perhaps she doesn't know what she's doing.'

He touched her fingers before standing.

'Or she's using it as a warning.'

They returned to Olly and left the death behind them, continuing until they saw the end of the road and the City of Dreams ahead.

'I thought it would be more impressive,' Jack said.

They got off the elephant together, and Ella peered at Pandora's new home.

'I expected skyscrapers and bright lights, or at least a castle and a few mansions.'

Instead, it was a collection of wooden huts with a street of mud running down the middle.

'It's not quite how it was described to me,' Olly said.

Ella stared at the shacks, hearing movement inside and wondering what Pandora had created that still lived. The smell of cooking drifted out of one, that stink of fried flesh that always made her feel sick. She was clutching at her stomach when an old woman wandered out of the closest hut.

'At least we've found something alive,' Jack said.

As Ella stared at the woman, she wasn't sure. She was dressed in rags and used a stick to walk. As she got nearer,

Ella saw the lines and scars on her wrinkled face. When she spoke, her voice resembled broken glass.

'My name is Sybil and I was like you once.' The stick creaked beneath her ancient fingers. 'Young and full of life, but look at me now.'

Jack stepped towards her. 'How long have you lived here?'

The old woman's eyes glazed over as she looked between him and Ella.

'At least a week.'

'Do you know how you got here?'

'Here? I've always been here. I was born here. That's all I know. My mother knows the rest.'

Invisible claws scratched at Ella's stomach.

'Where's your mother?'

Sybil lifted the stick with great difficulty and pointed down the street at the large building at the end. It was the only one made of stone.

'The Mother of Everything lives in Her church. That's where we worship Her.'

'How old are you?' Jack said.

'I told you, a week.'

Ella's heart sank.

That's what she meant when she said she was like me.

Jack took Ella to the side. 'I think whatever Pandora creates doesn't last long. All those bodies we saw on the way here,' he glanced at the woman, 'and going from a baby to that in seven days.' He shook his head. 'I wonder what's wrong with Pandora.'

'Let's ask her.'

They set off towards the church. Jack was by her side while Olly stayed behind. Ella couldn't blame the pink elephant, wishing to avoid this confrontation as well, but she'd known it was coming as soon as she'd followed Pandora from Earth.

Only Pandora didn't know about Everywhere and the multiverse. And she'd been lost ever since.

Ella's fingers dug into her hands, ready for her final meeting with her ancestor.

22 THERE IS A LIGHT THAT NEVER GOES OUT

They strode down the street together, glancing at the other huts as their occupants came out to watch them. Like the woman, they were dressed in rags, their faces full of lines and scabs. They said nothing as Ella and Jack kept going.

They stopped two feet from the entrance and he turned to her.

'Still no plan?'

She'd thought about it, expecting her brain to work when she needed it the most.

'If Pandora is as weak as she seems, then we shouldn't need one.'

That's what she hoped.

They went up the steps together and she pushed the door open. Inside, it wasn't like any church she'd ever seen. There were no crosses or symbols, no pews or places to sit apart from one at the far end.

And that was occupied.

'It's nice to see you, my old friend. And you brought a rabbit with you.'

It was Dora sitting there, the girl who'd been Ella's friend not so long ago.

The girl who'd pretended to be her friend.

The girl who was Pandora.

She got out of the chair and moved towards them, wearing the same clothes Ella had seen her in last: jeans, a white shirt, and a blue jacket. There were no marks on her face, no signs of ageing and tiredness.

But her green eyes were weary.

'Are you Dora or Pandora?' Ella said.

'I'm both, Ella. You know that.'

Ella shook her head. 'No. Dora was my friend.'

'I'm more than your friend, Ella. We are kin of the same blood. You are my granddaughter.'

Ella laughed. 'You said you're thousands of years old.'

Dora shrugged. 'Okay. You're my granddaughter a thousand times removed. It's the same thing. We are the same thing.'

'I'm nothing like you, Pandora. I'm not a murderer.'

It was Dora's turn to laugh. 'Isn't that why you followed me here, to kill me?'

'No. I'm no killer. I only want to stop you from returning to my world to take your revenge on humanity, like you promised.'

'And how do you intend to prevent me, Granddaughter?'

Ella gritted her teeth so hard, her jaw ached.

'I'll ask you nicely.'

Dora inched closer, and Ella noticed the fur on Jack's face trembling.

'It doesn't matter anyway, Ella. This is the end of the road for me.'

'What do you mean?' Jack's voice shook.

Dora held out her hands with the palms up.

'My Light is almost gone. On the way here, did you not witness the results of my failed experiments?'

'We did,' Ella said.

'That's all on you, Ella.'

'Don't blame me for your mistakes, Dora.'

'But they're not mistakes, Granddaughter. I don't have enough Light to create any life that lives beyond a few days because you took it from me.' She pushed her hands towards Ella's face. 'You stole it from me.'

Before Ella could respond, Dora had her by the neck, pulling the two of them to the ground. Ella grasped for her throat as they rolled across the ground. The rough surface irritated her as she struggled to breathe; every part of her ached as she saw Jack reach for Dora.

Then everything glowed yellow around them as an explosion threw him into the far wall. The blast tossed Ella away. Bells rang inside her ears as Dora moved over and peered at her.

'Return it to me, Granddaughter, and I'll let you and the rabbit go.'

Ella coughed before turning to spit. Her throat throbbed like a light bulb ready to explode. Then she glared at Dora.

'Even if I knew how to do that, I still wouldn't.'

Dora pushed Ella's hands away and sat on top of her, her weight pinning Ella down.

'It's ironic when I think about it. I spent thousands of years trying to escape from the realm which was my prison, and the first time I want to return there, I can't.'

Dora was heavier than she looked. Ella was twisting her legs to force her off, but failing miserably.

'You don't realise what you've done, do you?'

Dora pressed harder. 'What do you mean?'

Ella settled her back into the uncomfortable wood, knowing she wasn't going anywhere soon.

'This place, Everywhere, you didn't know it existed, and when you tried to return to your realm, with your body weakened, you found yourself here. And somehow, you changed everything, dragging bits of land and towns and cities into somewhere they shouldn't be. Thousands of years inside a prison you turned into your Queendom made you lazy. You made mistakes, and that's why you're here.'

Dora turned up her top lip. 'Yes, sitting here controlling you.' She scratched at her chin. 'But you're right, this place is new to me, and I took a wrong turn somewhere. But with your help, I'll return to my Elementals, and I'll feed on them until I'm at my full strength.' She glanced across at Jack's unconscious shape. 'The creatures here are not suitable for my digestion.' Then she placed her hands on Ella's chest. 'But you're just the snack to give me a boost.'

Her fingers dug into Ella as she screamed.

'Get off me, Dora.'

She kept on pushing. 'Not Dora now, Ella, only Pandora. I promise it will be over quickly, Granddaughter.'

Strength seeped out of Ella, her life swimming into Pandora in the form of a golden glow flowing from one girl to the other. A fire burned inside her brain, her flesh and bones boiling like the sun. Her insides shrivelled and she wanted to drink an ocean and feast on a forest.

I should have killed her.

It was the last thing she imagined before the pink trunk smacked Pandora in the head. The so-called Empress fell from Ella and rolled over.

'Are you okay?' Olly said.

Ella nodded. 'Check on Jack.'

The elephant trundled over to the rabbit as Ella staggered to where Pandora lay flat out on her back. She saw the shimmering gold hovering above her and wondered what to do next. She held out her hands for inspiration, and the golden glow, all of Pandora's Light, flew from her and into Ella. She didn't move, her body vibrating with energy, sensing it behind her eyes and feeling it sinking into her flesh and bones and blood. When Pandora was draining her, she was a deflating balloon, but now it was as if her insides were a bottle full to the top: it was a thousand times greater than how she felt when dancing in the air above the penguins.

Jack was frozen to the spot, staring at her.

'That's not something you see every day.'

Ella watched him rubbing the nape of his head and knew what she had to do.

'Come here, Jack.'

He did as instructed as she stood. She got him to bend over and placed her fingers on the back of his neck. What came next was as natural to her as sleeping or walking. Light flowed from her and into him. It lasted only five seconds. She removed her hands, and he straightened up.

'I feel fantastic. How did you do that?'

Ella showed him her palms.

'All of Pandora's Light is in me now, and it's growing by the second.'

Olly strolled towards them, swinging the trunk she'd used to knock Pandora out.

'You're different now, child.'

'I know, Olly. And thanks for saving me.'

'No, I mean you look different. You're glowing all orange and hot like the sun.'

'She's right,' Jack said.

Ella's hands shook. 'I'm overheating.'

She imagined being stuck inside a microwave on full power.

Concern filled the rabbit's face. 'What should we do?'

'Throw a bucket of water over her,' the elephant said.

Ella marched towards the door. 'I know what to do.'

She barged outside and the others followed her. As the Light increased through her, she ran into the centre of the town. People stood on either side of her as she took a deep breath before throwing her arms out, with her hands pointing east and west. She didn't have to think about what came next, letting the Light flow out of her in great bursts. It shot from her fingers and into all the people.

The sky lit up above her, a glorious orange and yellow column which flew from her body. She stood like that for sixty seconds, with everyone connected to her as if they were wires and she was an electricity socket.

Then they all collapsed together.

'Ella!' Jack shouted as he ran to her.

She was warm when he got there and took her in his arms. The glow had disappeared from her, but she had a massive smile on her face.

'I feel like I've just been to the toilet.'

'Nice,' Jack said as he let her go. 'I wonder how they feel.'

The people stood, still wearing dirty clothes, but changed beyond belief. Ella watched as they touched their faces and gazed at the others around them. They were young now; older than her, but much younger and more fresh-faced than before.

Ella wiped the dust from her trousers.

'I'm glad it worked.'

Jack stared in amazement. 'You healed them all.'

'Yes.'

Ella watched the people, saw the astonished looks on their faces and noticed the differences in ages, from early twenties to mid-thirties. At least, that's what they looked like to her. She wasn't sure how the Light stopped at a certain age for each of them.

'Did you use it all up, the Light?'

She shook her head. 'No, far from it. I think it was dying inside Pandora, but it's the opposite in me.' She smiled at the people embracing each other in joy. 'And I can do a lot more with it as well.'

'Such as?' Jack said.

'I know how to return home.' She went to him and took his hands. 'I know how to get us both home, and more.'

He stared into her eyes as the Light travelled from her to him. The surrounding air shimmered yellow and gold, with a smell of honey filling the sky. The people she'd changed for the better stopped congratulating each other and gazed at them. Even Olly came out of the church and waved her trunk in excitement.

It lasted for only a minute before Ella finished.

Jack peered at the glow coming from his paws.

'What have you done?'

'You can heal your daughter now.' She put a hand on his shoulder. 'I'll miss you, my friend, but you need to return to your family and save Olive.'

His lips trembled as he spoke. 'How do I do that?'

She grinned. 'I realised when Pandora had hold of me, could see it in the dark corners of her mind, what she'd forgotten about the Light.'

'What was that?'

She released him. 'All you have to do is picture where you want to be, and the Light will do the rest.'

Jack threw his arms around her and they hugged for a minute before he let go.

'How can I ever repay you, Ella?'

Before she could reply, a familiar voice chastised her.

'Is this how you're going to waste my gift, Granddaughter?'

Ella turned to Pandora. Or was she just Dora now? Ella smiled as she spoke.

'I'll use the Light for good, Grandmother.'

Dora narrowed her eyes, looking like a petulant teenager.

'And what about me? Will you leave me here?'

Ella glanced at the people Pandora had left to die as they observed the end of the drama.

'I'm sure these folks will treat you a lot better than you did them.'

Dora scowled and stamped her feet into the dirt.

'Don't worry,' Olly said. 'I'll ensure she keeps out of trouble.'

Ella knelt to hug the little elephant.

'I wish I could take you with me, but I don't think my world is ready for talking elephants yet. Even pink ones.'

They laughed as Dora stormed back into the church.

'Shall I go first?' Jack said.

Ella smiled at him. 'Why don't we do it together?'

They stood only a few feet apart as she stared at him, but thought of home, of her parents and Billy. As the world around her faded, she would have sworn she heard Dora scream.

Jack and Olly disappeared from her view, and, for a brief worrying second, all Ella saw was darkness. A chill stabbed at her heart before the light returned, and she realised it was a sea breeze biting at her flesh. As she looked up, she recognised the familiar construction in front of her, the one where she'd had so many adventures.

A wave slipped over her shoes and dribbled on to her toes before she jumped out of the wet sand.

That was her pier, but was she home again, or was this just another version of the town?

'Ella!'

She swivelled on her heels to see Billy running towards her. Then he bundled into her and they hugged as if they'd been away from each other for years.

'Billy, is that you?'

He let go and grinned at her through ice cream-stained teeth.

'Of course it's me, Ella. Who else would it be?'

She shook her head and laughed. 'I've been away for so long, I wasn't sure.'

He narrowed his eyes in confusion. 'What do you mean? You only went yesterday.'

Ella shivered, but she knew it wasn't from the cold.

'I'm back home and it's only been a day?'

She removed the phone from her pocket and saw it had the correct time. Billy stood grinning at her as she checked the photos on her mobile.

'I've got some fantastic things to show you, Billy.'

'Me too,' he said as he grabbed Ella and dragged her off the beach.

'Where are we going?' she said.

'You'll see.'

He held on to her hand as he pulled her past the amusement arcade and on to the pier. It wasn't busy, with only a few people staring at the sea, but she recognised the two standing at the end. Billy let go of her and she rushed to them.

'Ella!' Gemma Finn shouted as her daughter ran to her.

They threw their arms around each other as her father stepped towards her. He carried something in his arms, but she couldn't quite make out what it was with her head buried in her mother's chest. When she let go, he'd put it on to a bench. They hugged before she came up for breath, and she smiled at both of them.

'I've got so much to tell you,' she said.

'And we've got things to tell you, Ella,' her mother said. 'We've decided to stay here. We need a change from living in London. What do you think?'

She glanced at Billy standing behind her.

'That's great, Mum. But what will you do?'

Gemma looked at her husband. 'We're still going to be scientists, but we want to run a small farm here; one where kids will come and learn about the animals. And your father has just bought the first one.'

Ella watched him pick up the cage and hand it to her.

'I know you don't like seeing animals locked up, but this is only temporary until we get him home. He'll have lots of grass to run around on and can eat as many carrots as he wants.' She took the coop from him. 'What do you want to name him, love?'

Ella stared at the animal and thought of her friend another world away.

I wonder if I'll ever see him again.

Then she grinned at the rabbit.

'I'll call him Jack.'

THANK YOU!

Thank you, dear reader for purchasing this book.

If you enjoyed reading about Ella Finn her journey continues in these books:

Ella and the Elementals
Ella and the Multiverse
Ella and the Monsters
Ella and the Dreamers

Many thanks to my wonderful wife for all her support and patience.
Ella and the Multiverse edited by Alison Jack.
Extra special thanks to Karina Gallagher for being a dedicated reader of my work.
Cover design by James, GoOnWrite.com

ABOUT THE AUTHOR

Andrew French lives amongst faded seaside glamour on the North East coast of England. He likes gin and cats but not together, new music and old movies, curry and ice cream. Slow bike rides and long walks to the pub are his usual exercise, as well as flicking through the pages of good books and the memoirs of bad people.

Find out more at www.andrewsfrench.com

Facebook:

https://www.facebook.com/A-S-French-Author-150145625006018

Twitter:

www.twitter.com/andrewfrench100

Instagram:

www.instagram.com/andrewfrench100

And replies to all his email at mail@andrewsfrench.com

If you have the time, please leave a review at Amazon or Goodreads

Thank you!